Donated by
Floyd Dickman

MAKE ME OVER

Make me over

**11 original stories
about transforming ourselves**

Edited by MARILYN SINGER

● DUTTON CHILDREN'S BOOKS ●

DUTTON CHILDREN'S BOOKS
A division of Penguin Young Readers Group

Published by the Penguin Group • Penguin Group (USA) Inc., 375 Hudson Street, New York, New York 10014, U.S.A. • Penguin Group (Canada), 90 Eglinton Avenue East, Suite 700, Toronto, Ontario, Canada M4P 2Y3 (a division of Pearson Penguin Canada Inc.) • Penguin Books Ltd, 80 Strand, London WC2R 0RL, England • Penguin Ireland, 25 St Stephen's Green, Dublin 2, Ireland (a division of Penguin Books Ltd) • Penguin Group (Australia), 250 Camberwell Road, Camberwell, Victoria 3124, Australia (a division of Pearson Australia Group Pty Ltd) • Penguin Books India Pvt Ltd, 11 Community Centre, Panchsheel Park, New Delhi - 110 017, India • Penguin Group (NZ), Cnr Airborne and Rosedale Roads, Albany, Auckland 1310, New Zealand (a division of Pearson New Zealand Ltd) • Penguin Books (South Africa) (Pty) Ltd, 24 Sturdee Avenue, Rosebank, Johannesburg 2196, South Africa • Penguin Books Ltd, Registered Offices: 80 Strand, London WC2R 0RL, England

Library of Congress Cataloging-in-Publication Data
Make me over: 11 original stories about transforming ourselves / edited by Marilyn Singer.—1st ed.
v.   cm.
Contents: Some people call me Maurice / Joyce Sweeney—Not much to it / René Saldaña, Jr.—Bedhead red, peekaboo pink / Marilyn Singer—Vision quest / Peni R. Griffin—Wabi's ears / Joseph Bruchac—Honestly, truthfully / Terry Trueman—The resurrection / Jess Mowry—Bazooka Joe and the chaos kid / Norma Howe—The plan / Marina Budhos—Lucky six / Evelyn Coleman—Butterflies / Margaret Peterson Haddix.
ISBN 0-525-47480-3
1. Coming of age—Juvenile fiction. 2. Young adult fiction, American.
[1. Coming of age—Fiction. 2. Short stories.] I. Singer, Marilyn.
PZ5.M2855 2005   [Fic]—dc22   2005002109

Published in the United States by Dutton Children's Books, a division of Penguin Young Readers Group
345 Hudson Street, New York, New York 10014   www.penguin.com/youngreaders

Designed by Heather Wood
Printed in USA   First Edition
1   3   5   7   9   10   8   6   4   2

TO MY FRIEND
AND MENTOR
MICHAEL CART

—M.S.

ACKNOWLEDGMENTS ● *Thanks to Steve Aronson, Jay Kerig, Amy Livingston, Sherri Winston (who gave me the idea for this anthology), Michele Coppola (without whom it wouldn't have happened), Maureen Sullivan, Stephanie Lurie, and everyone else at Dutton, and to the amazing writers who contributed such great stories to this book.*

CONTENTS

MAKE ME OVER

● *by*
Joyce
Sweeney

SOME PEOPLE
CALL ME MAURICE

I'm late for fourth-period French. I spent too much time in the bathroom trying to flatten the front part of my hair. I figure there's just some little unimportant detail that's keeping me in this category I hate—the "like a friend" category. That's what I've been hearing since my freshman year. "Oh, Michael, I really like you . . . as a friend." Sometimes they're even cruel enough to use the word *love.* They *love* me like a friend. Love *this,* you picky little . . . but I digress.

The second bell rings. I pound rubber in the deserted hall. This is the last thing I want—to rush in late, all sweaty and flustered. As I run, I give off a breeze that makes all the little flyers for the Homecoming Dance flip up in the air. Like the whole corridor is giving me the finger.

I throw open the door of Room 213. Once my True Home, now a battlefield for my insecurities, thanks to Amelia (Angélique) McGovern.

Everyone turns to stare at me as I stand in the doorway, panting and sweating. Amelia is wearing a sweater the color of cranberry juice that makes me want to cry, it's so beautiful with her blue eyes. I feel the front part of my hair, an entity with its own will, spring back the way it was.

"Bonjour, Maurice," says Monsieur Rothstein, in his tired voice. He's one of those perpetually tired teachers, you know what I'm talking about. *"Vous êtes en retard."*

That's not as bad as it sounds. He's just pointing out that I'm late. I wrench my eyes from the cranberry sweater and shuffle to my regular seat, all the way in the back of the room, by my buddy Jake (Jean-Claude) Cacciatore.

"Bonjour, Retard!" he whispers. You have to forgive Jake. He's one of those really short guys who compensates by always trying to be funny. I'm one of those tall, gawky guys who tries to compensate by always being nice. We deserve each other.

I show my affection by throwing an elbow into his ribs and turn my attention back to Angélique. She's new, just transferred from private school, which adds to her mystique. She looks like a ballerina, all willowy and graceful with this faraway look in her eyes. Usually she wears pastels, so this shot of deep color mesmerizes me. Psychic, she turns around and gives me one of her curvy, closed-mouth smiles. I try not to get excited. She's just feeling sorry for her *en retard* friend. But today, unless I chicken out, which I probably will, I'm going to try to change all that.

"What did you do to your hair?" Jake whispers.

"Shut up."

We go way back, all the way to second grade. It was Jake who realized we could turn French Club into a haven for artsy, borderline nerds and make a niche for ourselves that's so weird and bohemian, it stays outside the pecking order. We wear Eurotrash fashion, we read Sartre and Baudelaire, we drink coffee instead of soda, and we dismiss anything the cool kids do as *bourgeois*. In short, we avoid the predators by behaving so strangely, they consider us inedible. It's a great strategy and good for our egos, too. We're somehow beyond social definition. And we all believe that someday we will be great artists of one kind or another when the football players and cheerleaders are buried in the *ennui* of their dead-end jobs and screaming babies. As Jake once put it, we've taken our sour grapes and made wine.

"Now that Maurice has been kind enough to join us," drones M. Rothstein, "we can enjoy yet another episode in the lives of those lovable kids from *Toute la Bande*. Please try to control your hysterical enthusiasm as I tell you that today's episode is called 'L'Anniversaire de Georges.' And remember to hold your applause till the end."

We laugh politely at M. Rothstein's sarcasm—this is all he has to keep him going—and he racks up our video *du jour*. Here in the lofty realms of fourth-year AP French, we are expected to be so fluent that we can understand ordinary French people as they converse. To test that dubious theory, we have to watch this series of films, clearly produced in the 1960s, about a rollicking group of Parisian girls and boys called *Toute la Bande*. After the show, we have to write up a little synopsis of what we've seen, to show we understood the story *parfaitement*.

As promised, today, our hero, an incredibly handsome kid named Georges, is having a birthday. He's *dix-sept* today, and is hitting the cafés with his fun-loving nonsexual friends. As always, we marvel that in our mecca, Paris, underage people can swill the *bierre* to their hearts' content. After getting drunk, *La Bande* playfully tells Georges they have a surprise for him.

"*La prostitute*," whispers Jake.

But no, they take him to this old lady's house, and she leads them all down to the cellar. Just when we start thinking something good is going to happen, like a mass murder of *La Bande,* we discover that the old lady has a dog who just had puppies, and, of course, one of the adorable *chiens* is Georges's surprise. The only part I can't understand is that they all keep saying *"malade"* and it doesn't look like anybody's sick, but I weave it into my essay anyway.

Lunch is the most important component of French Club. Oh, sure, we have meetings and yearbook photos and stuff like that, but the real French Club is our lunchtime, when we sit under the big poinciana tree in front of Palm High and show that we are a separate country from the cafeteria and its caste system. We bring Eurolunches: bread, cheese, fresh fruit. When we feel flush, we sometimes walk to Starbucks and get *un café.* Jasmine, who gets the lead in all the class plays and throws herself into her roles, sometimes gets French pastries to share with all of us. We discuss suicidal French poets and world politics as if we knew what we were talking about. It's a blissful interlude most days.

But today my stomach is in knots because I'm going to break our inviolate code of Being Above Dating and ask Angélique—I mean Amelia—if she'll go to the Homecoming Dance with me. I think first I'll ask her to go for a walk, away from the others. That will be shocking enough for a first step, and if I get scared, I can make up something else I wanted to talk to her about.

Everyone else is already under the tree by the time I get there, which starts Jake chanting, *"En retard! En retard!"* at me. It takes him a long time to get tired of things.

The girls are sitting in a row, like the Three Graces. Amelia is flanked by Jasmine (Josette) and Brianna (Babette). Jasmine, the thespian, is a curly-haired gypsy type who giggles her way out of all difficult situations. Bri is, by contrast, a deadly-serious, intense girl who plans to be an investigative journalist. The sixth member of our group is Robert, whose name doesn't change in French class (except in pronunciation). Robert is an artist, mainly a sculptor, who hardly speaks but is brilliant when he does say anything. Most of us think he's gay, but so far, if he is, he's keeping that to himself. Or from himself.

Bri unwraps a croissant. "So that was like the easiest episode we've ever had to do, right?"

Jasmine bites an apple. "Yeah, they should really give us something more challenging."

"Like dirty French movies," Jake suggests.

The girls all roll their eyes. When Jake's around, there's always a lot of eye rolling.

"It's kind of weird they gave him a sick puppy," I venture. "And what was supposed to be wrong with him anyway? He was barking and jumping around and everything."

Everyone stares at me. On some level I knew it, knew I had heard something really wrong. Why today? "They kept saying, *'malade,' 'malade,'* right?" I say. "Right?"

Jasmine and Jake both explode in fits of laughter. Bri looks disdainful. Amelia looks away. So Robert has to answer me. "Marmalade," he says quietly. "Marmalade was the puppy's name."

Maybe I don't need to go to any stupid dance or ever have love in my life. I mean, really. So for the next hour I just eat my lunch very quietly and let my dumb mistake dissipate into the air. Luckily, everyone is scared of some trig test we all just took, so that dominates the conversation. Since I'm good in math, I tune out and only tune back in when I hear Bri say, "Have you guys seen all these people making fools of themselves over this dance?"

Everyone gets energized immediately. Bashing popular kids is our most important function. "I wouldn't go to a dance if you paid me," says Robert, with a little too much venom.

"It's a meat market!" Bri says. "I can't believe in this day and age, girls are still willing to display themselves in those objectifying dresses."

"Which who can afford anyway?" Jazz puts in.

"If I tried to dance with most girls, my face would be in their chest," Jake begins.

Before he can think of the punch line, Robert makes the save. "The money they waste on that stuff is criminal. All those idiots should have to work in a soup kitchen for a week, so they could appreciate—"

"I'm thinking of going," says Amelia.

Everyone freezes as if she's pulled a gun.

"What did you say?" Brianna demands.

"What's the big deal? It's a dance. It could be fun. Do we have to be so serious about everything?" Her lovely eyes are calm but steady as she stares into Bri's challenging glare. Blossoms blow around them in the wind. It looks like a battle on Mount Olympus—Athena vs. Aphrodite, the brawl to settle it all.

"I totally agree with you, Amelia," I say, astonished that the Fates are giving me this opening.

She rewards me with her curvy smile. "Thank you, Michael. In fact"—she tips up her water bottle to get the last drops—"Bill Chastain asked me this morning. And I'm thinking of saying yes."

Oh, cruel Fates. Why do I trust you every time? I let out the breath that I had gathered to ask her to go for that little walk. Bill Chastain. A football player. A clod. A bore. An earnest, well-meaning dolt who will treat her right and get her to marry him and be the father of her beautiful children, who should be mine.

"I'm going to take a walk," I say, standing up so abruptly, it startles everyone.

"What's wrong?" Jake calls after me.

"Je suis malade."

People do all different kinds of things when they feel bad. I walk. Obviously, this is a healthier choice than Oxies or vodka or bringing weapons to school, but I don't do it to be virtuous. I do it because it works. My bad thoughts build up inside me like tornadoes, swirling faster and faster until I have to move my body to release the energy.

Today, Saturday, with the stupid, *bourgeois* dance just one week away, my bad thoughts are swarming like bees, so I take off right after breakfast and walk five miles to the Coral Square Mall. I keep picturing Amelia and Bill, dancing close under one of those disco balls (do they even really have those at dances? I wouldn't know). She's wearing a ballet dress and toe shoes. He kisses her. That's Bad Thought Number One.

Bad Thought Number Two features me in college, still trying to get my first date, tagging after groups of girls who scurry to get away from me, hugging their books to their chests like shields. I literally chase them, pleading. "We like you as a friend!" they scream as they break into a run.

Bad Thought Number Three—I am walking toward this mall because I am secretly hoping I'll find Amelia here buying her dress for the dance, and somehow we'll run into each other and fall in love. And I know that just by having that fantasy, I am now qualified to be the most Pathetic Guy Who Ever Lived. Pleased to meet you.

My sneakers seem to smack the sidewalk. We in the French Club know that the Parisian kids we admire subsist on the most minimal of wardrobes—sneakers, a good pair of jeans, T-shirts (one white and one black), white button-down shirts, and a big black pullover (which we rarely get to show off in Florida). The girls in our group sometimes wear fluffy skirts and flat shoes, like ballerinas. Timeless style can be acquired at Wal-Mart, if you know what you're doing.

Since I'm feeling pretty low, I sort of let myself escape into a minifantasy. I'm not Michael Morehead, every girl's best friend: I'm Georges, the handsome devil with the marmalade puppy. I'm not in Coral Springs, walking under palm trees. I'm in Paris, on the Rue de Faubourg Saint-Honoré, walking under delicately blooming chestnut trees. The House of Pancakes becomes the House of Hermès. That's not a turkey vulture soaring overhead, it's a nightingale. It's a nightingale, damn it.

Like the loser I am, I cruise around the mall for hours, going into every department and formalwear store, hoping to catch a glimpse of my angel. Of course, I should really know better. Even though she wants to go to a dance, her soul is still too bohemian for this punk mall. She's at some cute little vintage store right now, picking out lacy skirts and fringy shawls. Things that dolt Bill won't even appreciate.

I think my blood sugar is getting low. I'm starting to see visions, like a sign over the Food Court that says ABANDON ALL HOPE, YE WHO ENTER HERE. Ignoring the warning, I head to the Burger King booth and get myself a hamburger and some *frites.*

Adding to my torment, the only empty table is near a trio of giggly, taffy-haired cheerleader types, the kind Jake would kill to go out with. Luckily, I know I will be invisible to them (girls like that don't want friends), so I sit down. Since I am invisible, I watch them. They seem to be tussling over one of those big giant boxes of makeup samples you always see around Mother's Day. It stands to reason they'd all want the same color—they look enough alike to be sisters or clones.

I dive into my *Whoppeur* like a starving man, enjoying the waves of heated cologne scent that come from the cheerleader table. I picture myself sixty years from now, an old man on a park bench, getting whatever he can from just smelling the girls nearby. And just when I think I can't really get any sadder, the pot of lip gloss the girls were fighting over flies up into the air and bounces right off my head.

"Merde!" I shout. Me and my friends all curse in French because at least half the teachers don't know what we're saying.

The cheerleaders are all frozen, staring at me with identical sets of doll eyes. It appears that they were getting ready to laugh at me, but my foreign expression stunned them, like a powerful incantation. And that, my friends, is how easy it is to fall into a parallel universe. Given the choice of being a public *fou* or a mysterious stranger, what would any of you choose? And so, when I lean down to retrieve the lip gloss (lavender, sparkly), I alchemize into Georges again.

"Qu'est-ce que c'est?" I demand of the girls. *"Vous m'avez frappé!"*

The one with the most hair streaks (which I think makes her alpha) speaks first. "I think he's French!" she cries to the others.

She says it in the exact tone Jake would use to say, "She's a supermodel." *"Oui,"* I say, switching smoothly to the familiar. *"Tu parles français?"*

"Un peu," she says, pronouncing it "pooh." First year, I would guess. Most definitely not AP. *"Tu parles anglais?"* she asks me.

Do I? I think I probably should, given her skill level. *"Un peu."*

On some unseen command, all three get up at once and come to my table. I've seen flocks of birds do that. "I'm Crystal," says the ringleader. "And this is Jade and Amethyst."

Yikes! They're all minerals! I don't comment on that, though. French boys have impeccable manners. *"Je m'appelle Maurice,"* I say with a little dip of the head. Even my body language has changed.

The Three Minerals are drinking in every detail of me, from my Fossil watch to my "good" leather belt. If they know French fashion, they will find no detail out of place. Me and my *poseur* friends do our homework.

"Are you from Paris?" drools Jade.

"Oui. Rue de Rivoli." That just popped into my head. Probably something left over from world lit, maybe where Victor Hugo or some other deadweight lived. *"Je suis"*—I pretend to struggle for the right word—"in exchange."

"An exchange student!" Crystal translates. "So you're staying with an American family?"

"Yes. They are so nice. But they watch so much TV!"

The girls laugh. I am *très amusant.*

"Do you like America?" asks the third girl. Quartz? Schist?

I frown as if thinking hard. "I like some of the things . . . other things . . . not so much."

The girls are mesmerized. You'd think I was giving the Gettysburg Address.

"What don't you like?" Crystal wants to know.

"Well . . ." I gesture as I search for the words. It scares me, how good I really am at this. "In the high schools . . . all the social classes . . ."

"Social studies? That's in middle school," says Jade. It's sad that she knows less English than me, a poor immigrant.

"No, no, I mean the social . . . order. The cliques, the labels

Americans put on everyone. Everyone is judged. It is so . . . petty." Yes, I know, I've called them cheerleader types several times. That's different.

"That's just the way it is." Crystal is bored with my social views. "What do you like about America?"

I prop my chin on my fist like a guy who knows he's cute. "The girls are soooo pretty!"

They giggle, and I flash my eyes at them. It's amazing, like some kind of wonderful demonic possession. I'm not just pretending to be capable of flirting. I *am* capable of flirting.

"We're going to the beach in a minute," says that third one. Dolomite? Conglomerate? "Want to come?"

I hesitate. I'm not sure I can pull off this *charade* for an extended period of time. Plus, I'm wearing a black T-shirt. And I don't have any sunscreen with me. I smile my dazzling French smile. "I'm afraid I cannot. You see, I'm engaged."

"Engaged!" cries Crystal. If anything, this has added to my appeal. I'm a hottie who can commit.

"Is that the wrong word?" I ask sweetly. "I'm going to be married to a girl in France."

"No." Jade sighs deeply. "That's the right word."

"What's she like?" Crystal asks, like a little kid at story hour.

"Oh, she's the most beautiful girl in the world. Her name is Angélique. She's a dancer, a ballerina." Then out of nowhere I add, "I'm going to be a novelist."

"Wow." Jade sighs. "She's so lucky,"

"No. I am the one who's lucky."

Crystal lays her French-manicured hand on my arm. "Your fiancée wouldn't mind, Maurice. We're just going to hang out, get some sun, no big deal."

I ask myself, *What would Georges do?* "Okay." I nod vigorously. "Yes."

······

Ten minutes later, I'm cruising down A1A in Crystal's blue Mustang convertible, mesmerized by the sight of three shades of blond hair flipping and flying in the wind. If only there were some way to get a movie of this. Because Jakey will never believe me when I tell him. I struggle to stay in character and speak like a foreign tourist. "You Americans are so lucky," I say. "You have your own cars. You can just drive to the beach. From Paris, I have to take the train." I draw this information from *Toute la Bande episode cinq,* "A la Plage."

"But you live in Paris!" says goggle-eyed Amethyst, who shares the backseat with me. "What do you do for fun with your friends?"

"We go to cafés or dance clubs," I say. "Mostly we just hang up."

Crystal looks over her shoulder. "Hang up?"

I frown with puzzlement. "Hang in?"

All three girls explode with laughter. "Hang out!" says Jade.

I laugh along. "Oh, yes, of course."

What a wonderful novelist I will be.

We lie in the sand on a big blanket Crystal keeps in the trunk of her car. The girls all have swimsuits on under their clothes. I try to remember as they strip that I'm from a country full of beautiful women, and there's no need to stare. They all produce bottles of cocoa butter from their canvas bags. I let them persuade me to take off my T-shirt, and we oil each other up. I've never even had a dream this good.

I pretend we're on the Riviera. I'm a spoiled rich kid who can't decide among my three girlfriends. Through my eyelashes, I

Joyce Sweeney

● SOME PEOPLE CALL ME MAURICE

watch them scamper in and out of the water, sparkling like the gems they are.

After a while, Crystal produces a flask. Kamikazes, she says. I understand the name after about three sips. As the sun and the flask get lower, everything starts to sparkle even more. I feel like I'm inside a soap bubble, encased in rainbows, floating farther and farther away from the loser I thought I was.

Monday, I come back to school with a killer tan and a different point of view. Today, Amelia is wearing her ballerina outfit. I look at her differently, too. My glance doesn't bounce off her and land on the floor. I look at her deeply, study her hands, her jaw-line, her waist.

I can't explain why being in a fantasy world over the weekend has somehow made reality much more real. Or maybe I mean the opposite. Because now I know that even though Amelia is planning to be a doctor, and she's never taken a dancing lesson in her life, she really *is* a ballerina. And that I really *am* a novelist.

And I know we belong together.

So when I walk up to the French Club at lunch and say to Amelia, "Will you take a walk with me?" even though everyone else freezes, she just smiles, gets up without a word, and follows me.

We walk halfway around the building, holding hands. I don't feel like Georges, or Maurice, or even myself. I feel like someone I've never been before. "Do you have to go to that stupid dance with that stupid Bill?" I look her straight in the eyes. "Because I want you to go with me."

She stops and leans against the building. The wind plays with the edges of her hair. Her eyes are like a lake on a cloudy day. "I was waiting for you to ask me, Mike. But you didn't."

I can see myself reflected in her beautiful, peaceful eyes. And then I realize something really huge. The new way I'm seeing myself—she saw me that way all along.

"Is it too late for me to ask you?" I run my finger down the side of her face.

"No, I didn't give Bill an answer yet."

"Good." I put my arm around her, and we walk together. I see out of the corner of my eye that she's sort of staring up at me. "What?" I ask.

"What did you do, Michael? There's something about you that's . . . different."

I stop, take her hand, and kiss it. *"Vive la différence!"*

● *by*
René
Saldaña, Jr.

NOT MUCH TO IT

Becky had only last week graduated from the McAllen College of Beauty Arts and Sciences and immediately found work at Cuts and More. Today she was at the bookstore picking up a how-to manual on manicures and fingernail polishing. She walked up to the customer-service counter and saw it was Chela working. They'd been kind of friends all through high school. Kind of. More like Chela and her group of girlfriends let Becky hang out with them because she was enrolled in the School-Within-a-School program and studying hairstyling. They were part of the A group and getting asked out all the time, so they had Becky do their hair, for free. "Practice," they called it. "We're actually helping you improve."

She knew better. They were taking advantage of her, plain and simple. Sure, the girls were nice enough to her; while she worked on their hair, they talked about their dates (who was the good kisser, who wasn't, who left the bigger tips at restaurants, who had the best manners, etc.) and let her into their circle in that way. But Becky knew she was only partway in. She heard the condescension in their casual chatting with her; she saw it in their turning to whisper the real juicy secrets to one another; she felt it in their too-tight hugs after their hair was cut and styled. Becky put up with it, though, because there was always the chance that they'd receive her into their midst. It was a long shot certainly, but a shot nevertheless.

It wasn't until close to finishing school that she began to realize she could never be one of them, no matter what. She wasn't a cheerleader or band member or an honors student; she was never pulled out of classes to meet with college recruiters; she wasn't being asked out by the captain of the football team, the first-chair sax player who performed a solo to a standing ovation at last year's Pigskin competition, not even by the guy who scored a near perfect on the SATs. Oftentimes, especially there toward the end, she had to remind herself of the sad reality: They all loved the work she did with their hair, and that's how she got to hang out with them. She'd be done with school in no time at all, she'd think, *and* with them. *They'll be out of* my *hair soon enough,* she liked saying to herself.

Then they'd throw her a curve, and she'd be back to imagining how great it would be if they thought she was cool enough for them. It had been Chela, for example, who'd put the idea into Becky's head to keep studying after high school: "You've got a knack for this, Beck. Not just anyone can do hair. You need to share your gift with the world." That's how these girls talked, always big, always grand. But Becky appreciated Chela's words of encouragement, and three weeks before high school graduation, she called up MCBAS and asked for an application packet. They told her that finishing her program at the high school would be enough. She'd be licensed. But she wanted more, not just a high school diploma like everyone else. She insisted, and after talking to several people there, she'd been accepted. Now, after an intensive three-month-long stint in salon management, she'd gotten a second diploma. It said she was board certified like her high school one did, but this one said "college," and now she felt prepared to work in the beauty industry.

"Hey, Beck," said Chela. "What you up to?" She was absently turning the pages of a magazine, a stack of books for reshelving beside her on the counter.

"Oh, hi, Chela," Becky said. She hadn't seen Chela or the others since graduation night. They'd gone to their parties, and she'd sat at home. "I'm here for a book I ordered. Can you check if it's in?"

Chela typed Becky's name into the computer, and a window popped open. She said, "Be back in a sec, Beck," and in a few moments was walking to the counter with the book. She was flipping through it, smiling.

Becky remembered that patronizing smirk from back in high school. She thought, *I can't believe this. She's laughing at me. How dare she? I mean, look who's got a career—me—and who's got a summer job—her. And what's with the hair?*

"This it?" Chela said, showing Becky the cover.

"Yeah, that's the one." Becky thought, *And there's that ugly tone in her voice to go with the look.*

"Anything else I can help you with? A book on pedicures, or hair coloring?" Chela smiled.

There it is again, Becky thought. She was sure of it. Chela poking fun at her chosen vocation. Like being a beauty technician was beneath her, but schlepping to the back of the store to get a book for someone else wasn't servile? Standing behind a desk and answering phones wasn't menial? *Whatever,* Becky thought.

I'm going somewhere. I've got my five-, ten-, and twenty-year plans already charted out. She's hawking books.

It disturbed her, though, that try as she might, she'd never impress these girls. Her being in the workforce, not just passing the time at a temporary job until Daddy started paying for college, but busy in legitimate, lifelong employment—it amounted to nothing with them. She hoped that after school, things would've been different. They'd all be grown-ups and behave like it, but it was apparent today nothing had changed. And this bothered her. Becky was even more upset because caring what Chela thought still today made her stomach get all in knots. She figured she'd gotten over her insecurities after graduation. Obviously not.

All the same, she did have plans. One day she'd manage Cuts and More. Later, she'd open her own place, call it Becky's Beauty Boutique. She'd even printed out business cards on her computer: All the *B*s in bold and in pink, then under that her name, also in pink, followed by *Proprietor,* and under that, *Board Certified.* No address or phone on them yet.

But right now she took her manual; pictured on the cover was a thin hand with long, painted fingernails. She said, "Thanks," turned to leave, then spun back around and said, "Chela."

Chela looked up from her magazine and smiled.

Becky took a deep breath, then said, "Chela, you might think about coming to see me at work soon. You really need to stop doing whatever you're doing to your hair. I'll put you on my Preferred Client list, give you a free shampoo."

Chela's smile cracked almost imperceptibly, but enough for Becky to notice. "Really—a free shampoo? How nice of you! I had no idea salons charged for a squirt of Pert and rinse water. But as you know, I haven't been to a real salon in at least four years."

"Do stop by. You'll be glad you did." Becky swung around and headed to the register.

In her car, her book on her lap, Becky couldn't believe she'd said what she'd said to Chela. In high school, she'd never've dared. She would've been ostracized, a leper to everyone.

But what had possessed her to do it today? She was in a kind of shock, confused because she'd always been hurt when someone had humiliated her like she'd just done to Chela, but as lousy as she felt about doing it, she was also proud for having stood up to the likes of her. *I mean, to offer to put her on* my *list,* she thought, *not the other way around.* Never mind there was no list, really. She looked at herself in the mirror, smiled, and wondered, *The new me?*

Becky put the car in gear, turned up the volume on the radio, and drove home. The rest of the night she tried reading through her manual. There were all kinds of helpful hints on how to prepare hands for manicures, what soaps and creams to use or not depending on skin type, how to strengthen fingernails, and a chapter devoted to the myriad ways of applying fingernail-polish designs for different occasions. But Becky couldn't concentrate. She was still shaken by how she'd behaved with Chela. She couldn't get the look on Chela's face out of her head: discomposed for once, unsure of herself; her eyebrows raised, the shaky smile, and the shade of pink on her cheeks. At which point, Becky'd spun and left.

What bothered her more than how Chela had looked was that, even now, a few hours later, she still felt good about how she'd acted. She knew from back in high school these girls were all about the latest fashion; they'd told her about how new dresses or hairstyles had gone largely unnoticed by dates and how ungrateful guys were: "We go to all this trouble for them, and what thanks do we get? Not even an honorable mention!" Becky thought, *And what thanks did I get?* They'd whimper on that way for a good while until Becky told them the same thing every time: "Listen, you're beautiful. This is how guys are programmed. They're genetically engineered to skip over such details. They just don't get it." The girls always seemed to agree and smiled. She thought they were such big crybabies, though. So she knew earlier today that she'd crossed a line with Chela. For better or worse? She didn't know.

But so what? Chela'd never introduced her to the popular guys. Not once did the group invite her to a party where she could meet them on her own. She was never on equal footing with them. Sure, they'd invited her to sleepovers, but that just meant she'd have to haul her makeup kit and her styling tools and spend the night attending to them. Giving them the works. Why had she ever wanted to be part of them? Even tonight she couldn't figure that one out. And she couldn't fall asleep for thinking about it all.

In the end, she told herself, all she'd done today was to behave a little like them. No harm done, really. She turned out the light and fell into a rocky sleep.

At Cuts and More the following morning, she was tidying up after her previous client. She bent to sweep all the hair into the oversize dustpan, then she looked up and saw Chela signing her name to the list at the counter. She scooted back a bit, stayed bent that way, out of sight behind her chair.

What's she doing here? Becky wondered. She waddled back-

● NOT MUCH TO IT

ward, saw Chela was making a call on her cell, and shot for the employee lounge at the back of the shop. *Really, what* is *she doing here?*

She considered the possibilities: maybe to complain to Monique, the manager, about how one of her techs had had the gall to criticize her hair in public; maybe to get her hair done, then make a stink about how Beck got it all wrong and demand to get it for free (like in the old days); or maybe, just maybe, she'd agreed with Becky's assessment and was here for a fix-up? The split ends really were too noticeable, too readily seen. Monique had probably immediately noticed them, too. *So that must be it, then,* she hoped.

She snuck a peek out the door and saw Monique talking with and smiling at Chela. Monique pointed at Becky's station, then she looked puzzled. *Where could Becky be? She was just there,* Becky imagined her saying.

Then she actually heard Monique: "She may have stepped into the back room. Lemme go check. Sit right here, hon," she said, and pointed at one of the recliners in the shampoo station. She was smiling. "If she said it's free, then it's free."

But when she headed to the lounge, she was shaking her head.

What could that mean? Becky jumped back and dumped the hair she'd swept up earlier.

"Becky," Monique whispered, "nothing in life's free. Well, almost nothing. One thing that is, though, is a shampoo." She raised her eyebrows at Becky. "Why'd you tell that girlfriend of yours you have a Preferred Client list and that she's on it, and that she gets a free shampoo? I don't approve. That's misrepresentation, you understand?"

"Yes, Monique. It won't happen again. It's just . . . I read in a book at school it's a way to entice potential clientele. Make them feel special, and—"

"Sure, get them in the door, and you got a customer for life. I didn't have to read that in no book. Nor go to school. But it's plain falsehoods you're telling this girl. We on the same page? Now get out there and wash that girl's hair, style it, and be done with it. Take your lunch early, why don't you?"

"Yes, ma'am," she said, and her heart was beating hard.

"Well, get out there already. Your friend's waiting on you."

Becky took a breath and wiped at her sleeves, where she could see tiny, almost unnoticeable bits of black clippings from her last customer. Her forearms'd already begun to itch. She checked her face and hair in the mirror by the door and stepped out.

"Hello, Chela. I didn't think you'd come." She wondered if she should apologize. "Glad you did. Hey, about yesterday . . ."

"Think nothing of it, Beck. Really, once you left, well, out of sight, out of mind, right? But after my shower this morning, I looked in the mirror and had to agree with you. My hair's dreadful. I just hadn't noticed, but to a trained eye like your own . . . ? I mean, what with your degree in beauty and stuff, you mustn't be able to walk down the street without picking out bad and good hair. That's some serious talent. You must think we're all slobs."

Becky wanted to say, *You mean my two degrees,* then point to where they both leaned against the mirror, but instead said, "No, it's not like that at all." But why was she backpedaling, balking, caving in? "Shall we?" was all she could muster. She wished she were quicker, wittier. More sarcastic. She so wanted to cut Chela down, but couldn't. She grabbed a bottle of shampoo.

Chela said, "Do with me what you will. Make me into something I'm not, if you think you can. I put my hair into your care."

Becky smiled. That was good, what Chela'd just said: *Put your hair in my care.* Nice. Maybe she'd type it up as her slogan on her business card, make posters of it to put up when she owned her own store: *Real nice.*

"I'm meeting Jimmy after, and I want to look good. So we need to hurry. Let's do it to it."

"Sure, let's start. Just lie back."

"You did say this part of it was free, right? What with going out of state for college, I've got to save every penny."

"Sure. You're on my Preferred Client list, like I said. Free shampoo, every time."

"Good. Ah, that warm water feels so good. You seeing anyone, or are you still on the market? Don't wait too long, Beck—nothing uglier than a wilted flower. But don't worry, Mr. Right'll come along, someday."

When Becky didn't answer, Chela asked, "Why didn't you ever shampoo us when we were in high school? That would've been the cherry on top, you know."

Becky shook her head—"I don't know"—and rinsed the last of the lather from Chela's hair. She began to massage the nape of her neck like she did for all her clients, but she noticed how Chela stiffened. She didn't open her eyes, and she didn't say anything, but Becky knew to pull back her fingers. She grabbed for a towel to dry her hands. She remembered working on Chela's hair one sleepover, the others looking on, a running commentary of *oohs* and *aahs*. When she had tried gathering her hair in a bunch and lifting it over her head, Chela had gone rigid the way she'd done today.

"I like my hair loose and bouncy," Chela'd said.

"Loose and bouncy, just like you," said one of the other girls, and they all giggled, Chela included.

Later, she'd asked Becky to come into the restroom to help with some eyeliner.

Becky found her near tears. After several minutes of trying to comfort her, Becky put an arm around her shoulder.

"Okay," Chela said, and wiped at her face. "This is just between friends, right? You can't tell anyone else, promise?"

"Of course I promise," Becky said. She'd never heard a single one of these girls use the word *friend* in reference to her. "It'll be okay."

Chela bunched up her hair and hesitantly pushed it up off her neck. "How embarrassing," she said, and let Becky take a look, then confessed she didn't know how to deal with all the acne. "Any idea how to get rid of it?"

Becky had recommended rubbing aloe straight onto it; she wasn't sure, but aloe wouldn't hurt.

The following Monday at school, Becky handed a bottle of aloe to Chela between classes, behind the lockers, where no one could see them.

Chela took the bottle, looked at it, then shoved it back, saying, "What's this?"

"It's for the—you know," said Becky, pointing to the back of her own head.

"Don't worry about that. I'm going to a dermatologist who'll give me real medicine. Not this Farmer Brown, home-remedy stuff."

Becky didn't understand. At the sleepover, Chela had called her a friend, made her promise to keep a secret, cried, let Becky hug her in comfort. "But—but I was just trying to help a—"

Chela cut her off: "Help? Please, you're studying to be a beautician. I swear, if you say anything about this—" and she stomped away.

Becky'd stood at the lockers holding out the bottle of aloe until the bell rang. She'd wanted to cry.

Today, Becky dried her hands and handed Chela a towel. "Done with the shampoo," she said.

She led Chela to her chair, wrapped an apron around her, covering her lap, chest, and shoulders, and asked, "So, what shall we do with it?"

Chela answered, "I'm at your mercy, but not too short."

In about half an hour, she was done with Chela's hair. She'd cut it short, but made sure it was down past the neck. It was one thing to tell Chela her hair was horrible, quite another to hurt her that other way. "What do you think?" she asked, unwrapping the apron slowly. Then she let all the wet clippings drop to the floor at her feet.

Chela looked in the mirror, pursed her lips like prunes, looked this way and that, asked for a hand mirror, studied her hair from behind, and smiled. "This looks great," she said. "I'm a new woman." She ran her fingers through her hair. "What do I owe you? You're such a good beautician I'll even pay for the shampoo. Better than in high school."

Becky couldn't win. Not today, not ever, so she told her the price of the haircut and reminded Chela she was on Becky's Preferred Client list, so not to worry over it. The least she could do was kill her with kindness.

"Well, in that case, I'll tip you what it would've cost to get my hair washed. What do you say to that?"

"You don't have to tip. After all, we're friends, right?"

"Nonsense, Beck. You did great work for me today; Jimmy'll love it; you deserve something. Think of this as a little token," and she handed Becky a crumpled ten-dollar bill out of her back pocket. "Money's money, right. We all can use it." She looked at herself in the mirror again, then said, "I just figured out why you didn't go all out like this back during our sleepovers—we never tipped you. I bet if we had, you would've done it all and more for us. Why didn't we tip you back then?"

"Friends don't have to tip friends," Becky said. "So, here's your money back."

"Don't be silly. How else do you girls make a living except for the thoughtfulness of your Preferred Clients?" She turned and started walking to the door.

When she reached it, she turned and said, "Wouldn't it be great if we could go back to those times? All of us—you, too—and you could do wonders with our hair *and* nails, with your new book and all. We'd tip big. I'd make sure of that. It would all be different, if only . . ." She smiled, ran her fingers through her new hair again, pushed the door open, and said to no one in particular, "This girl deserves a raise; she's an artist. I'm keeping you a secret all to myself, though," then stepped out of Cuts and More.

Jimmy, her boyfriend from high school, was waiting for her in the parking lot. She jumped into his truck, leaned over the armrest, and kissed him on the cheek. Becky watched them as he backed out of his space, shifted gears, and drove away.

Go back? she thought. *Not for ten bucks; not for a million. It would all be different, my big, fat toe.* She walked back to her station and swept up all of Chela's hair that had fallen there. She thought she'd cut a good deal of it off, but in the dustpan it looked flimsy, and there wasn't much to it. So she dumped it in the back room with everybody else's hair they'd cut today.

• *by*
Marilyn
Singer

BEDHEAD RED, PEEKABOO PINK

At seventeen, Tom Flinch had already learned that the world was full of people who loved to make pronouncements, all of which were contradictory.

"The meek shall inherit the earth," his father liked to say.

"Only the strong survive," his mother would mouth.

"Only fools fall in love," was his brother Miles's motto.

"Love is all you need," was his sister Theresa's.

"'Life, like a dome of many-colour'd glass, stains the white radiance of Eternity,'" his other sister Augusta would quote. Nothing seemed to contradict that one because nobody (except the poet Percy Bysshe Shelley, who wrote the thing) knew what it meant.

Tom's best friend, Clancy, who was pretty much a member of the family, had as his favorite catchphrase "Any guy can get a date."

Tom himself was the walking contradiction of that creed. He'd never had a date in his life. And it wasn't for lack of trying.

Which was what they'd been talking about one hot July morning at the public swimming pool, both of them scanning the bobbing bodies, Clancy with anticipation, Tom with pessimism. Then he noticed the dark-haired girl in sunglasses sitting on a towel, a straight white cane at her side, and said, "Maybe *she'll* go out with me."

Clancy glanced up. "You are kidding, right?"

Tom hadn't meant to speak aloud. But it was too late now. "No," he replied flatly. "I'm not."

"But she's blind!" Clancy exclaimed.

Tom resisted the urge to tell him to lower his voice. "Yeah," he said instead. "Exactly."

Taken individually, Tom's features were okay—brown eyes, somewhat droopy; auburn hair, thick enough to cover his slightly pointed ears; broad forehead; snub nose, wide mouth, narrow dimpled chin. His teeth were crooked, but at least he kept them clean. He was tall and a little stoop-shouldered, with large hands and feet. His clothes were baggy and beige. Nothing about him by itself was repugnant. But taken as a whole, Tom had, in his grandma's words, "A face only a mother could love." In short, he was ugly.

Kerry Whittaker had written it in her notebook way back in seventh grade.

Two years later, somebody else—a male or possibly even a daring female, he'd never found out which—had scrawled it in the boys' bathroom.

And two months ago, Lindy Sloane, the *freshman for God's sake* he'd asked to the junior prom, said it to his face. "I'm sorry, Tom. You're a nice guy, but you're . . . you're . . ."

"Weird-looking?" Tom prompted.

"Well, uh, yes," Lindy had agreed, then quickly added, "No offense."

"None taken," Tom had lied. He'd been quite offended. He'd been offended, too, the day he'd read Kerry's notebook, conveniently left open on her neighboring desk in history class. He'd never stopped being offended.

Every book, movie, TV show, or fairy tale preaching that it was inner beauty that counted fell on deaf adolescent ears. In real life, nobody believed the frog would ever turn into the prince.

Tom found himself starting to rise when the girl, cane in hand, came toward him. Her hair was naturally curly. She had prominent cheekbones and thick eyebrows that might've met in the middle if not for careful tweezing. Her arms and legs were long and muscular, and her bathing suit was a particularly vivid pink. She was what Tom's dad would playfully call a "looker."

"Hi," he said as she neared.

She nodded and kept going.

"Wait!" He jumped up, took her arm, and began to lead her in the opposite direction, toward the locker rooms.

She yanked her arm away so hard that he nearly tripped. "What the hell do you think you're doing?"

"You were h-heading toward the p-pool," he stammered.

"Really? Now who would've thought they'd put a pool in here."

Tom was normally a bit slow when it came to sarcasm, but not this time. "Oh," he said. "You swim . . . ?" Then, worried that she might take offense at that, too, he added, ". . . well?"

She cocked her head. "Yes. Very. Do you?"

"Not really," he said, with such mournful honesty that she smiled a little. Like him, she had a dimple in her chin, but on her, it worked. "Maybe you're not spending enough time in the water." With that, she turned, walked to the lifeguard's chair, stuck her sunglasses on one of its rungs, propped her cane next to it, and dived into the pool.

She wasn't lying—she was a superb swimmer.

"Hot damn," said Clancy, watching her.

Tom stared down at his skinny freckled legs and let out a big sigh.

Two days later, clutching a bag of incisors and molars, Tom decided to take a quick shake break. Next to the dental lab where, as his new summer job, he picked up and delivered crowns, bridges, and other assorted false teeth, there was a brand-new drugstore with an old-fashioned soda fountain. His dad had read the ad about its opening at a recent "brunch" (which was what Mrs. Flinch called their haphazard weekend breakfasts because none of them, except Tom, got up before ten) and declared it "A damn clever idea. Novelty for you kids and nostalgia for old farts like me."

Tom decided his dad was probably right. The pharmacy had bright modern lighting and shelves, a gleaming counter with multicolored bar stools resembling oversize golf tees, and a jazzy riff that played each time a customer entered or exited the store. But the menu was pure fifties. Tom was about to park his narrow butt on one of the stools when he heard a girl say, "Bedhead Red, excellent choice."

He turned. There, at one of the registers, handling a lipstick, was the blind girl from the pool.

"Um . . . thanks," the customer replied awkwardly.

"I've used this one myself," the girl went on, "though I prefer Peekaboo Pink. It goes better with my coloring."

For the briefest moment, Tom wondered if she was faking either her blindness or her taste in lipstick. The woman clearly didn't know what to think either. She laughed hesitantly, then handed over a bill. "It's a twenty," she said.

The girl ran it under some sort of scanner. "So it is," she said. "And not a counterfeit one either." She rang up the purchase. In a robotic voice, the register announced the change due. The girl gave it to the customer, who didn't bother to check it, just stuffed the money in her purse and left the store.

"Well, she won't be back in a hurry," a man, graying and handsome, called over the high pharmacist's counter. He had a slight accent. Italian, maybe, Tom thought, or Greek.

"Who cares?" said the girl.

"I, for one, do. Can't you go a bit easier? This is only our second week of business."

"Okay, okay. Maybe—for you." The girl had an impish smile. So did the pharmacist, as well as the same prominent cheekbones and bushy eyebrows.

Are they related? Tom asked himself. Perhaps that was why he'd hired her. Tom had never seen either of them before—not that he knew everyone in town, but he thought perhaps they'd moved there recently. However, he wasn't about to ask. He looked at the door wondering if he should go, but he could almost taste the shake, and it was a trek to the nearest Dairy Queen. *Besides, she'll never know I'm here,* he told himself, *will she?*

Quietly he made his way to the counter, sat down, ordered, and thought about his plans—or lack of them—for the evening. He and Clancy had talked about going bowling tonight for a goof. Clancy said it was the stupidest sport in the world (next to curling). Out loud Tom always agreed with him. In truth, he liked bowling. It was the only sport he was any good at (if you didn't count thumb wrestling, at which he and his long thumbs excelled). But Clancy had canceled. He had a last-minute date. A blind date, set up by his cousin Patrick. "I owe him," Clancy had said, but he didn't sound all that perturbed about it.

The blind girl stirred him from his reverie. "This yours?" she asked. She was standing next to him, holding his satchel with two fingers. He'd absentmindedly set it on the adjacent stool.

"C-careful!" he stammered. Any breakage and he'd be out of the best-paying job he'd ever had.

"Why? Will it bite me?"

"Heh. As a matter of fact, yes."

"Really?" The girl cocked her head. "What's in there? A rat? A spider? A Chihuahua?"

"None of the above," Tom replied.

"One chocolate shake." The soda fountain waitress, a fair-haired wisp of a young woman, set down his drink in front of him. "You want one, too, Cara?"

"Sure, why not?" said the girl. "I'm not watching my weight. I let other people do that for me." She smiled her impish grin. Then, loudly, she announced, "Besides, I'm entitled to a break."

The pharmacist heard and snorted. "So am I, but am I getting one?"

Tom took a swig of his shake and licked the foam off his upper lip. Cara was still facing him, her sunglasses reflecting back his face. "Well, what then?" she said, nodding toward the stool.

On impulse, Tom opened the satchel, took out one of the bags from inside, and held it out to her. "Go ahead. Put your hand in. Carefully."

She didn't hesitate. Rooting around, she felt the contents—an upper plate of dentures—and laughed. "I see," she said. Then, giving back the bag, she said, "You were the guy at the pool yesterday, weren't you?"

Damn, how'd she know? Must be my voice. "Yeah," he admitted. "Sorry about that. I didn't know . . . I didn't think . . ."

"Most people don't," she said, but her tone wasn't nasty.

Tom relaxed a bit. "You really are a good swimmer. Are you good at other sports, too?" As soon as he said it, he felt embarrassed. What other sports could she be good at? Baseball? Soccer? Boxing, for God's sake?

"Bowling," she said.

"Bowling! That's my sport. But how do you . . . I mean . . . how can you tell . . . I mean—" He stopped, hugely embarrassed. She was grinning, letting him hang himself. Oh hell. He took a deep breath. "Would you like to go sometime?"

"Depends," she said.

"On what?"

"On what you look like?" she answered.

He blinked. "Pardon me?"

"I don't go out with ugly guys," she explained. "You know, poor little blind girl, all she can get is a dog. I don't even like dogs." She laughed at her own joke. "Are you blond? I like blonds."

Out of Tom's entire family, he was the only person who always told the truth. Lying literally gave him a physical pain. But now he rubbed his chest and tried to ignore the stabbing sensation. "B-blondish," he stammered.

"Blue eyes?"

"Yeah."

"And how are your teeth?" She grinned.

"Perfect," he said.

"I'll bet," she replied. She paused. "Okay. How about tonight?"

"You'll go?"

"I just said so. You can pick me up here at eight. That okay?"

"Y-yeah." He finished his shake in three more gulps, slapped down some money, and fled before she asked about his nose, his ears, his chest hair, or his legs, and some other fib escaped his lips.

She was standing outside the store, feeling her watch. He chewed at his lip. He was fifteen minutes late and covered with dirt. "I'm so s-sorry. Flat t-tire," he stammered. "I tried c-calling the store. Got an answering machine."

"Next time, try my cell," she said.

Next time? *I hope there is a next time,* he thought. But, encouraged, he asked for a pen and wrote the number she rattled off on his already-ruined T-shirt.

"Car's across the street." He hesitated a moment, then offered his arm. She took it by the elbow. His bare skin tingled. He hadn't been touched intentionally by a girl since seventh-grade dance lessons.

He guided her to the car but let her seat herself. They drove along in semicomfortable silence. He made a right turn, then another, then a left.

"Aren't we going to Melody Lanes?" she asked. Melody Lanes was the big state-of-the-art alley near the mall. Tom had been there a few times, but he much preferred Paradise Alley, just outside of town. It was older and shabbier, but few kids from school went there. It was the perfect place to be unseen. He wondered how she knew about Melody Lanes—and she told him. "My uncle—he's the pharmacist—and I have been going there a couple of times a week after work since we moved here two months ago."

It was the first bit of personal information she'd given him, and he held on to it as carefully as the bags of teeth he delivered. Then he replied, "Uh . . . there's a place I like better. . . . Is that a problem?"

She turned, as if studying him. "Not yet," she said.

Cara had her own bowling shoes, which she kept at the pharmacy. Tom did not. As the guy behind the rental counter handed him a pair, Cara asked, "You have the new 'Bowling for the Blind' thing yet?"

"Nope. Got a guide rail, though."

"Well, that's something."

"Last lane on the left."

"Thanks."

"You'll have to be the pinspotter," Cara said to Tom when they reached the lane.

"Okay," he said, watching her carefully select a ball.

Sliding her hand along the guide rail, she took three steps and rolled it down the lane.

"Number ten standing," Tom said.

She adjusted her position and made the spare. "Yes!" She pumped her fist in the air, then turned to him. "Don't you damn well hold back!"

"I damn well won't," said Tom, and they both laughed.

Tom won, but not by much. He couldn't remember having ever enjoyed bowling so much. It was a relief to play with a real competitor. He wondered what else she was good at, what other surprises she'd have in store.

It wasn't the only thing he was curious about. That night in bed, he couldn't sleep for all the questions he wished he could ask her: Had she been born blind? Did she see only blackness? What did color mean to her? What about ugliness or beauty? What did she picture when she met people? What did she dream? And how the hell could she tell the difference between those lipsticks?

Then another question popped into his head—a big one: *What happens if she finds out what I really look like?*

The question wouldn't let him sleep. At 4:00 A.M., he had the answer—he wouldn't go out with Cara ever again. But the answer gave him no relief. He got out of bed and made his way in the dark to the family-room computer, banging his shin twice in the process. He was planning to read some of the stuff on the Web that he never got around to because his siblings were always online, but his attention was drawn to his e-mail. He didn't get much, if you didn't count the spam. The subject line of this note said "Spare me!" He recognized the address at once—Cara had given it to him six hours ago. How she read and wrote e-mail was another mystery he didn't expect to solve.

He tried unsuccessfully to squelch the twinge of excitement as he opened the note and read:

> *My favorite bowling jokes:*
> *1) I hear that small town used to have a bowling alley—*
>   *until somebody stole the pin.*
> *2) I'll never bowl with that quarterback again. Every time*
>   *he gets a strike, he spikes the ball.*
> *And last, but not least (drumroll)—*
> *3) "Something is wrong with my bowling delivery," Tom*
>   *said gutterally. (barrump-bump!)*
> *Friday night, same time (minus fifteen minutes), same*
>   *place?*

Tom reread the note three times (partly because he didn't immediately get the last joke). At four-fifteen he had a new answer: He would go out with Cara again; as long as they kept bowling at Paradise Alley, they'd be safe.

• • •

Augusta, who found him draped over the keyboard, asleep at last, woke him to say that Clancy was on the phone. Tom yawned hello into the receiver.

Clancy sounded way too chipper. He asked if Tom wanted to go to the mall after work. "Gotta get some new duds," he said.

Duds. "Grandpa speak," as Tom called it, meant something unexpected and possibly embarrassing had happened. He took a guess: "Patrick's girlfriend's cousin. Debt not only paid, but it paid off."

"She's kind of cool," Clancy admitted.

Tom had planned to tell Clancy about his date, but suddenly he didn't want to. He was afraid that might jinx it. Instead he said, "Maybe I oughta get some new duds, too. Ruined my good T-shirt changing a flat."

"Which one's your good T-shirt? The one that says *Chow Main Restaurant* or the freebie from Slater's election campaign?" Clancy teased.

"Ho ho," Tom said, declining to tell him it was the one from Winesap Cider Mill, where he'd worked last summer.

At the mall Tom watched his friend pick out a pair of pants, two shirts, and some silky boxer shorts. "Jeez, you've only gone out with her once!" he said.

"Never hurts to be prepared," Clancy said.

Tom shook his head, then took a bright blue polo shirt off the rack. "Think I'd look okay in this?" he asked.

"You?" Clancy said, surprised. "Yeah. You'd look okay."

Tom nodded and pulled out his wallet.

"You mean you're actually going to buy it?"

"Yeah, my parents taught me it's wrong to steal," Tom replied jauntily.

Clancy stared at him suspiciously, "Is there something you're not telling me, Flinch?"

Tom heard Cara's voice in his head. "Not yet," he said.

He wore the shirt on Friday night. Also Saturday and Sunday (having washed it in between). He was right. They were safe at Paradise Alley. Safe and . . . well . . . there was no other word but *happy*, was there? It wasn't just the bowling. It was the talking. They talked about all kinds of stuff, from music to politics to best brands of chocolate. Cara liked to "discuss" things. Tom thought *argue* was a better word. But he didn't mind because Cara really listened to what he had to say—made him say it, in fact. No one else had ever solicited his opinions before.

What they didn't talk about was Cara's blindness. He was even more full of questions. But she didn't bring it up, so neither did he. Occasionally she asked for help.

Occasionally—and carefully—he offered it.

Once, after a snack, he watched her skillfully apply lipstick. "Bedhead Red or Peekaboo Pink?" he asked lightly.

"Neither," she answered a bit shortly.

He let it go.

He was beginning to feel that they—he—were doing really well. And then, on his way to the lab, he closed the car door on his thumb. The sprain made driving tricky and bowling—and e-mailing—impossible. He racked his brain about what they could do instead and where they could do it.

It was Cara who suggested a movie, some new comedy at the Decaplex. With its long lines and lobby arcade, it was the worst place to go if you didn't want to be seen. He suggested the Foxview instead, as out of the way as Paradise Lanes.

"Okay," Cara agreed. He could hear the wariness in her voice through the phone.

The date went well, though. She didn't question how he was managing to drive even when he grunted once in pain. The theater was empty enough so that they disturbed no one the few times Tom had to whisper descriptions of what was on the screen. But afterward, when he pulled up to her house, she said, "My family would like to meet you. Can you come for dinner on Sunday? My folks are from Italy. They do those antipasti, primi, and secondi courses really well. The dolci are good, too."

His first thought was, *Wow, you actually have Sunday dinner? With your whole family?* His second was, *And have your whole family see me?* "Uh, sure," he said. "What time?"

On Saturday he went shopping again, this time alone. Stomach fluttering, he bought a dressier shirt and pants, and shoes, too. Cara was busy that night, and he wasn't sorry. On the way home, he ran into Clancy, coming out of the barbershop. Tom hadn't seen him in days. "Hey," Tom said.

"Hey," Clancy replied.

"You doing anything tonight?"

"Yeah," Clancy answered, a little sheepishly. "But tomorrow afternoon I'm free. Wanna do something then?"

Tom's stomach fluttered again. It was the right moment to tell his best friend about Cara. But he didn't. "Can't. Got a family thing to go to."

"Oh? Is it at your aunt Jo's?"

Clancy had gone to plenty of Flinch-family functions, and he loved Aunt Jo's cooking in particular. "No," Tom said. "No one you know."

"You've got relatives I don't know?" Clancy grinned.

Tom's return smile was rather wan.

"Listen, I'm sorry I've been so busy," Clancy said sincerely.

"That's okay. I've been busy, too," Tom replied.

"Sure," Clancy said, and it was obvious he didn't quite believe him. "Well, if Sunday's no good, how about Tuesday night?"

"Maybe. I'll let you know."

Clancy nodded. Then he saw his cousin across the street. "Gotta talk to him," he said, and was gone.

The next morning Tom slept really late. He got out of bed slowly, feeling like he was pulling himself up a ladder by his fingertips. He showered and dressed with equal deliberation, donning his new clothes as if they were made of paper. Combing his hair, he stared at his face. He flared his nose, crossed his eyes, puffed out his lips, then snarled. "Hell," he swore. "Hell, hell, hell!"

He took off his new shirt and pants and shoes, put on his oldest, baggiest clothes and battered sneakers, and reached for his cell phone. Dead. He'd forgotten to charge it. He went out into the hall. Theresa was on the house phone. She'd been on it for the past half hour. He knew because he'd heard her pick it up when he'd headed for the bathroom.

"Get off," he growled in a low voice.

She stared at him. "Excuse me?"

"NOW!"

She was so shocked, she obeyed.

He waited till she was out of hearing range and dialed Cara's cell.

Cara answered after one ring.

He made his voice hoarse. *Sorry . . . just woke up . . . bad sore throat . . . can't make it . . . Sorry,* he told her.

She told him that was a shame and they'd do it another time.

Sure, he lied. There wasn't going to be another time. He knew it. And by the end of the week, when he didn't answer her e-mails or return her calls, she'd know it, too.

Saturday morning Clancy showed up for brunch.

"I thought you and Patrick's girlfriend's cousin were going on a picnic," Tom said with newly developed gruffness as he let his friend into the house.

"She's got a summer cold, she says. But I think it's *OBB*," Clancy said gloomily.

"What the hell's *OBB*?"

"Old Boyfriend's Back."

"Dames," Tom said, sneering, putting his own spin on "Grandpa speak."

For a change, Tom's whole family was assembled in the kitchen (probably because Augusta—the only decent cook in the house— was making pancakes). Miles and Theresa, with their usual attempt at one-upmanship, were arguing, this time about cloning.

Cara would love this, Tom thought, feeling the by-now painfully familiar ache in his chest. He jiggled his leg and drummed on the table.

"What do you think, Dad?" asked Theresa, who appeared to be championing the Cloning-Good side, although Tom wasn't listening closely enough to be sure.

With practiced obliviousness, Mr. Flinch rattled the paper. "Look at this. There's a new place opening on Cookson—a salon for men. What say we get a facial, eh, Clancy?"

"Sure, Mr. F," Clancy replied. He was used to Tom's father's joking.

"Mom, what do you think?" asked Miles.

"Has anybody seen my glasses?" Mrs. Flinch responded.

Theresa and Miles clicked their tongues in contempt. No one noticed that Tom's drumming had gotten louder.

"'If the blind lead the blind, both shall fall into the ditch,'" Augusta, flipping a pancake, put in, though no one had asked her opinion.

Tom pushed back his chair so violently that it fell over. Without bothering to right it, he charged out the back door and into his car.

"Cloning," he muttered. "Who'd want to clone an ugly guy like me?" He drove aimlessly, head roiling, chest aching, eyes dry with self-disgust.

Then he found himself on Cookson. The street name scratched at his recent memory. He slowed to a crawl. Amid blocks of blandness, a shiny dark-green-and-cream building, hung with tasteful deep blue flags, stood out. Over the door, in the same deep blue, was the word URBANE.

Tom pulled into the lot and got out of the car. He walked determinedly to the window and peered through. Then, before he could change his mind, he went inside.

"Whoa!" said Clancy. He was sitting in Tom's old Taurus. Tom had explained nothing on the phone, just apologized for running out and asked Clancy to meet him at his car in the pool parking lot. "I can't believe it!" He'd been saying little else for the past five minutes.

Tom gave in to the urge to stare at himself in the rearview mirror. He couldn't believe it either. His thick auburn hair was now gelled, spiked, and streaked blond. His eyebrows had been plucked, shaped, and lightened. His skin, steamed and mud-packed, was glowing. His body, sauna'd and massaged, was straight but relaxed. His eyes were still brown and a little droopy—short of blue contact lenses, which he felt was going too far, there was nothing he could do about them. He still wasn't handsome—but now he wasn't a dog either.

"Your family's gonna flip!" Clancy declared.

"Her uncle says she has the day off," Tom responded. "He thinks she came here."

Clancy cocked his head. "Huh? Who?" he asked.

"Cara."

"Who's . . ." Clancy began. Then suddenly he knew. "The blind girl?"

"Yeah." Tom nodded, and a moment later, he poured out the whole story.

When he was finished, there was a long pause. Then Clancy jumped out of the car, ran around to the driver's side, and yanked open the door. "Out," he commanded.

Tom got out. Together they made their way to the pool.

Cara was there, along with the soda-fountain girl from the pharmacy. *Uh-oh,* Tom thought. His stomach flip-flopped. He turned, ready to flee. But the soda-fountain girl had spotted him. She whispered something to Cara. He watched Cara's mouth go from pursed hostility to wide-open surprise.

"Tom!" Cara called. "Get over here!"

"Go on," Clancy urged.

It was the longest few yards he'd ever walked. At the salon, he'd had lots of time to think of what to say to Cara, but now everything flew out of his head. What flew out of his mouth was, "I'm blond. . . . I wasn't, but now I am."

"I know," Cara replied.

"My eyes are brown, though. I'm not so hot-looking either—but I'm improving. . . . "

Cara's lips trembled, whether with amusement or some other emotion he wasn't sure. "Rikki, would you please excuse us?" she said to the soda-fountain girl, who rose reluctantly and dived into the pool.

"I know," she continued. "I mean, I knew . . . Rikki told me that day. . . . I'm really sorry. It was a joke, sort of, me and blonds. But true, too. About stereotypes, y'know. I thought you were asking me out because—" She broke off. Tom had never before heard her sound so halting, so abashed.

Taking a breath, she said with more deliberation. "I wanted to find out if and when you'd tell me the truth . . . and then . . . then I got to like you, and I didn't really care."

"But I care," Tom said quietly.

She nodded. "I see that now. But before, I didn't put it together. . . . I mean, I thought you didn't want to be seen with me—"

"You?" Tom said, astonished. The thought had never even crossed his mind that she might think that. "No way!"

She bit her lip and stood very still. Then she took off her sunglasses. Her eyes were the same color as his. They looked like regular eyes, but . . . blank. It would've bothered Tom, he had to admit, had he been meeting her for the first time. But now he could see through them to the dance and sparkle of her mind.

"Bedhead Red. Peekaboo Pink. Labeled them myself—initials, in Braille, under the price sticker," she said. "Easy to tell them apart that way."

It was an offering. Later he'd take her up on it, question by question. For now, he simply said, "Oh." Over her shoulder he could see Clancy checking out Rikki in the pool. He looked back at Cara. "So . . . you . . . uh . . . want to go bowling tonight?"

"Yes!" Cara said, so loudly several heads turned. "Yes, I would," she repeated in a lower voice.

"Okay, then." His voice bubbled. "Melody Lanes?"

"Uh-uh. I prefer Paradise Alley."

"Yeah? Me, too." He smiled. Running his tongue over his teeth, he wondered how much it was going to cost to get braces.

by •
Peni R.
Griffin

She walked down the steps of the school, and kept walking into
traffic. She heard Leti calling: "Hey, Liz!"

Am I Liz? Her head did not turn, her feet did not falter. Alex's
lowrider cruised at its usual five miles over the speed limit, honk-
ing, his sidekick leaning out the stuck window to yell: "Hey, Elizabitch! We gonna run you down!"

But apparently she wasn't Elizabitch, either, because she
didn't respond, and they didn't run her down. The other traffic
took no notice of her, and she continued down the gutter of the
side street opposite the school entrance.

The Savage Pomeranian on the left-hand corner charged the
chain-link fence, and on the right-hand corner, the football coach
and his flunkies prepared the field for practice. Matt, who had
bought her a gold necklace that said *Beth,* was probably in the
swarm of more or less burly boys pouring over the crosswalk, but
she didn't look to see. Matt was the smallest guy on the team,
guaranteed to be creamed if he was ever allowed to play. "I do it

because it annoys the coach," he'd told her, grinning, and she had grinned back, as if she'd understood.

"Yap yap yap yap," blustered the Pomeranian, threatening, presumably, to fluff her to death. Without breaking stride, she unhooked the necklace and dropped it, glittering, into the drift of leaves and pecans in the gutter. Her conscience twinged. If Matt knew she'd tossed it . . . ! She'd come back for it later—to keep it, or return it. How could she tell which, until she knew whether she was Beth or not? And how could she find that out, wearing what amounted to Matt's label?

In fairness to Matt, he hadn't meant it as a label.

So—she was someone who was fair to Matt? That didn't seem sufficient, even as a beginning. She shook her head, and her hair patted her cheeks.

Leti had chosen the hairstyle. "You've been doing the wrong thing with your face. Trust me." So she'd sat down in the beauty-shop chair, watching the blah girl in the mirror and wondering, *Who is that?* But when a cute girl emerged from under the hair, she kept on wondering. The hair was just Leti's label for her, and she couldn't drop it; so now she bent over as she walked, shaking her head, shaking the curl loose, then brought her head up again and combed through it with her fingers.

The Pomeranian left her when the chain-link gave way to the open front yard of a pink bungalow where a lady in a housecoat smoked, watched the football field, raised her hand, and said: "Hi. How you doing?"

Her stride did not break, but her hand went up and her mouth said: "My feet hurt. How're you?" as she went by.

So. She was a girl whose feet hurt.

She proceeded across the next intersection, kicking at the straps of her sandals until they were under her heels. Then she stepped out of them, with long strides, still on her toes. The gravel and stored sunlight in the asphalt bit her feet, so she hopped the curb and walked on the verge, mostly soft green, with hard spots of blond dead grass. Her feet, striped tan and white, flashed below her, questioning their freedom.

Mom would have a fit. She fussed if the kids went barefoot. Dave kicked his shoes off whenever he could get away with it and sulked through lectures about the need to protect his feet. Sure enough, he'd stepped on a rusty nail last year—tetanus shots, crutches, lots of groaning and drama and hogging the computer when he wasn't hogging the TV. These days he still went barefoot, claiming he was watching his step, making Mom crazy apparently on purpose. But if Mom was so interested in protecting their feet, why had she been the one to suggest high heels?

"Something dressy," Mom had said, though tennis shoes were acceptable with the public school uniform; and it was fun, the khaki skirt flipping around her knees, the heels raising her ever so slightly higher than the sea of heads. Dressiness drew her into the orbit of the rich girl clique. She was never one of them, but they asked favors, because they knew she was a Good Girl. Heads would have rolled over the cherry-bomb incident if she hadn't been available as an alibi; and the rich girls repaid her in parties. Yes, high heels had been good to her, and she'd probably wear them again, but they were not her.

The street made a T intersection with the road that paralleled the creek. She watched with interest to see which way she would veer. To her surprise, she continued in a straight line. The view from the top of the bank was intimidating; surely she couldn't press through so much brush? And what about when she reached the bottom?

Her heels would have made the slope impossible. She stepped

over a crumpled and faded Dr Pepper can and narrowly avoided a shattered longneck. Branches of huisache and dry stalks of Queen Anne's lace, fuzzy with burrs, snagged her skirt, her purse, her bookbag. She slipped, landing in a tangle of hackberry, reeds, and white plastic grocery bags, her knee cracking against a jut of limestone, her bookbag hauling her backward because it had caught on something sturdy with thorns.

"Ow, ow, ow!" She shook herself free of the bookbag and inspected her knee. She hauled herself upright, using a sapling as a crutch, and tested her ability to stand. The pain began to fade into an abstraction, annoying but livable. She brushed her skirt to get the burrs off and succeeded only in rolling them down the fabric.

The creek was dark, the water interrupted by mats of sticks and algae, plastic grocery bags caught on rocks, the round edge of a can. A current ruffled the surface toward the middle. The breezeless shade smelled funky—not a stink, exactly, but too warm and not exactly welcoming. She stepped forward. In response, the creek said "plonk," a semicircle of ripples spreading from beneath the vegetation along the edge, which was cool and slippery.

She watched her foot plunge into the dark water. The bottom was loose and silty, with a stick hard and fragile under her sole. A smell of methane rose as she put her weight down, pivoting so that the other foot never entered the water but landed on the bank. Her purse struck her sore knee as she reached for huisache to steady herself. The creek ran off her skin, leaving a patina of algal specks.

You idiot. You dropped your bookbag. It has your whole life in it!

She looked up the bank—more plants, more litter, more steep dirt—and climbed. Her bookbag held two notebooks, her science and English texts, a Spanish/English dictionary, pens and pencils, calculator, homework assignments, address book, calorie counter, granola bar, library book, and a hint book for *The Sims: Unleashed.* Was that really her whole life?

Limping, she arrived at the weedy patch between the creek and the access road and kept going. The cars on the road were far enough away not to be a danger. The man behind the guardrail stared over his cardboard sign that said ANYTHING WILL HELP. She reached into her purse and pulled out her lunch money, thrusting it at him as she stepped over the guardrail.

He made no move to take it. "Don't do it, honey," he said. "Whoever he is, he's not worth it."

What the—oh. She must look wilder than she'd thought. "I have to," she said, "but that's not what it's about, and I'm not doing what you think." She tucked the bills into the breast pocket of his camouflage jacket, dropping the change on the pavement, and kept going, under the overpass.

"I'll spend it on liquor," he called after her.

"That's up to you," she answered, crossing the stained concrete, past a three-wheeled shopping cart and a colony of pigeons, their gossip echoing as the highway that roofed their aerie shuddered under its burden of traffic. She sprinted over the exit ramp to the Diamond Shamrock on the other side safely—though a pickup honked at her.

It hadn't even been that bad a day. Lockers, gossip, gym, geometry, social studies, government, English, chemistry, and what was any of it about? No breakfast—she'd slept too late. No lunch—she and Leti and Brit had a date to run down to the drugstore and buy things for Brit's party, though Brit hadn't needed advice. She just didn't like going to the store alone.

She'd been thinking about Mr. Teachout's sidetracking discussion of coming-of-age rituals for days. Teachout was easy to distract. He'd only needed a little nudging to stray from the antihazing rules to initiations, to bar mitzvahs, to vision quests. "There didn't used to be any of this adolescent stuff," he said. "You were a boy, and then you did your ritual, and you were a man. Hunter-gatherer tribes typically sent their boys out on vision quests. Heading into the wilderness with nothing, no weapons or maybe one simple one, fasting, maybe climbing a mountain, maybe hunting a dangerous animal. Eventually you'd collapse and have a vision, where your totem animal gave you wisdom and the tools to survive; and then you were a man."

"What about women?" Leti had asked.

"They didn't need rituals," said Teachout. "They became women when they started menstruating." Which caused a nervous giggle to go around the room, like this was middle school instead of high school. "The point is, you get your vision, you kill your bear, you get your period—boom! You're an adult. None of this futzing around being an adult when it'd be an advantage to be a kid and a kid when it'd be an advantage to be an adult."

She had looked it up in the library, so she knew Teachout had not been 100 percent accurate. Sometimes initiations were group affairs, with lone vision quests reserved for shamans, and girls got rituals, too, sometimes just as physically demanding as the boys'. The main point was a good one, though—without the initiation you didn't know what you were, who you were. And getting your period didn't make you a woman, not anymore. She'd looked that up, too. When that was true, girls hadn't started bleeding till they were eighteen.

It explained a lot.

Someone with an unlimited supply of spray paint had created a rich, dark mural along every inch of the cinder-block wall of the strip shopping center she was passing—doves, flames, men in muscle shirts, and women in pseudo-Aztec regalia—transforming tempting expanses of taggable wall into a surface too complex to show any sign a gang wanted to put up. A beauty parlor flanked by jade-decked beauties, a dollar store with black vultures perched on its lintel, a taquería swamped by stampeding bulls. At the extreme edge of the building, where the sidewalk gave way to an asphalt drive mostly filled by a Dumpster, the artist had signed an illegible swirl of color, as three-dimensional as the feathered snake coiling around the corner. His name didn't need to be legible, she realized as she walked past the Dumpster (heavily tagged) and waited at the light. He knew he was the person who could paint that mural.

You are what you do, said her dad in her inner ear. If you drank, you were a drinker; if you did drugs, you were a junkie; if you stole, you were a thief. If you studied, you were a student; if you danced, you were a dancer; if you drew murals, you were an artist. She had provided the alibi for the cherry-bomb incident—ergo, she was a liar. But didn't telling the truth otherwise make her honest? What about poor Lourdes, who used to be in the good English class? Everyone knew Lourdes would rather read than hang with her "homeys" drinking beer, but the penalty for that was black eyes and broken noses. Was there a real Lourdes under the colors and scars, or had her big sister, by jumping her into the gang, robbed Lourdes of herself? What was the expiration date on identity?

If what you did was all you were, she was the girl walking barefoot past Bill Blanco's Allnight Allright Ice House and Laundry and getting whistled at, and in a minute, she'd be the girl walking barefoot across another street.

I am the girl worrying her friends and parents sick.

Initiations were supposed to be done by your society. Did they count, could they count, if you did them yourself?

Past the garage, across the street, past Diamond Shamrock and Fred's Fish Fry and a Taco Bell building with a FOR SALE sign in the window, under another overpass. She fell into a walking rhythm, taking long unvarying strides to the tune of her heart. Her fingers felt thick and numb, as if the blood were pooling in them, so she pumped her arms and cracked her knuckles as she entered a district of duplexes and small homes.

Downtown rose on the horizon, distant mountains of glass, and her purse strap chafed her shoulder. When people stared, she smiled.

I'm a girl on a vision quest.

I'm an idiot who's scaring her family for no reason.

I'm a crazy lady walking barefoot through town. I should stop now.

Yeah, then I'd know who I was—a wimp who couldn't finish what she started.

Isn't that better than being stupid?

The street dead-ended in a lot bisected by a concrete-lined drainage ditch. Grass scratched her legs, and she took extra-long steps to avoid the ant mounds. Nearby, but invisible, a dog barked and boys called, their voices shrill and unintelligible as those of the grackles sweeping across the sky. A rabbit darted away.

A rumble of wheels, and a boy flew up out of the drainage ditch, an inhuman figure with a board connecting his feet. Arms spread, he jumped in midair, reversed, and vanished below, greeted by more barking and the shouts of the other skateboarders. He hadn't seen her; none of them saw her until she started half walking, half sliding, down the sides of the ditch. Four boys and a yellow mutt, festoons of graffiti, and a dark streak of former floodwater down the center. "Look out!" shouted a boy, and the one headed straight for her did a too-quick reverse, fell, and leaped up.

"Sorry," she said. "Are you all right?"

They stared at her as she crossed the central channel. The dog growled and wagged his tail, his breath warm on the backs of her knees. A boy called it to heel as the fallen one said: "Uh—fine. Look where you're going."

"What do you want?" asked the fourth.

"Just passing through," she said, seeing him, knowing he was familiar, without pausing in her forward movement.

"Don't you go to my church?"

His sister was in her youth group, and his family usually sat one pew down and a little over. "That's right."

"Um—Betty, right?"

"More or less." The concrete scraped her feet and hands as she climbed/crawled up.

"Man, you look terrible," said the one who'd almost run her down. "Are *you* all right?"

"I'm on a vision quest," she said. "Can't stop. See you Sunday, um, Kurt."

"Oh, man, that is one weird chick!"

But she was already at the top, walking across more grass to the railroad tracks perched on a causeway of gravel paralleling the ditch. A train moaned far away, and the track bed hurt her feet. The ties, dark and sticky, smelled of creosote and the unfortunate opossum that had timed its own crossing badly, a few hundred yards down the line. Then more grass, another street, another neighborhood.

No sidewalks. Ranch houses, mostly with smooth lawns. A few xeriscapers had created minilandscapes, masses of Carolina jessamine, plumes of fountain grass, bougainvillea. No people in sight, but a few cars in the driveways—extras, occasional transport for stay-home parents, the clunker that took the oldest kids to high school.

She walked along, still waving her arms to work the numbness out of her fingers, wondering about totem animals. Presumably, a pet dog or cat wouldn't do, but what about strays? What about the grackles and white wing doves and sparrows crowding the birdfeeders in the xeriscaped yards? Were totem animals maybe not physically real, so she had a good chance of getting something cool like a bear or a cougar?

The street rolled over the terrain in long, slow waves, following the slope of the prairie beneath the subdivision. Maintaining her straight line would mean climbing chain-link fences and, in some cases, breaking through doors or even walls. Was it wimpy not to try? *You're overthinking it,* she thought, *whoever you are, you're a person who overthinks things instead of doing them, and whatever else does or doesn't happen today, that's changing. Trust your feet.*

The curve emptied into a zone of two-story apartments lining six lanes of traffic. The evening work exodus had begun, herds of silent, sleek monsters competing for blacktop. She stopped at the light and punched the pedestrian button, grateful for the rest provided by the inordinate wait for the walk signal. Did vision questers have to go without water until they met their totems? Probably not; they probably drank from the clear mountain streams and springs they encountered on the way. The lights above the crosswalk turned red; a final car dashed across before the impatient beasts lined up, their noses overlapping her path, and the walk light finally came on.

She had barely stepped off the curb before DON'T WALK began flashing urgently red. Head high, she walked past the snorting, panting ranks of commuters, achieving the sidewalk six lanes away as the light changed, and they charged onward.

Another commercial district, another residential one, and the glass mountains gradually swung around before her. The buildings and yards became insubstantial as light and color drained from them. Her thought processes drained out, too, and she could feel herself paring down to a body—mouth swelling paradoxically with the subtraction of water, empty belly shrinking and gnawing, viewpoint swaying with the motion of her weary legs, the ache creeping back into the knee she'd banged at the creek.

Even if she had turned her head, she probably wouldn't have seen the driver of the car that started to pace her, some sort of sedan in last year's fashionable color. She heard the whir of the window lowering easily despite the whoosh of the car that went around it. "Hey, you want a ride?"

No temptation to answer; you didn't have to be on a vision quest to ignore this sort of thing.

"Hey. You want a ride?"

Bears, cougars, wolves. At least they didn't pretend they were doing you a favor. Her eyes darted around for an escape route, but her body remained steady. Aunt Helen's advice had always held good in these situations. "All responses are encouraging to these jerks," she said. "See, they're only men if women are paying attention to them. So if they can get your attention, they'll never let go of it, no matter what. You don't have time for that."

"You want a ride? You want a ride? You *want* a *ride*?"

If nothing else, she had more identity than this guy.

"Hey, didn't your mother teach you any manners? I'm not trying to pick you up here. You *look* like you *need* a ride."

Besides, her mouth was so thick and numb with thirst, she couldn't have answered if she'd wanted to. A bus bore down on him, claiming its rightful lane.

"Stupid bitch." A bottle flew from the window past her face, but she didn't flinch, didn't even wonder whether it was intended to hurt or to frighten her, and he burned rubber through the next stop sign as the bus swept the smell of diesel past her.

Downtown was close enough that she couldn't see it as an entity anymore. Commercial and residential, downscale and upscale, bad parts of town, good parts of town—they seemed bigger and more distinct when she traversed them in a vehicle. The pace of her walk made it easier to see how small was the distance between the grubby grocery stores and the shiny corporate markets, between the historical district and the run-down older residences and the houses converted to bars and boutiques, between the streets she'd been taught to fear and the streets she'd been taught to shop. Her mother would have called the street where the boys started following her a "good part of town."

She didn't notice them at first, because they didn't whistle or catcall. They were just there, strung across the sidewalk, not too near, but not far enough. She pretended not to see them, but an edge of nervousness touched her when she saw a small urban park with a water fountain.

Water holes were where predators caught prey.

She *needed* a drink.

The fountain was old, with a star-shaped handle. The first turn shot a stream of water down the front of her blouse; reversing the tension produced a trickle that would have required sucking directly from the spout. At the third attempt, she gulped down warm water. She heard them approaching, talking about something besides her, laughing, daring each other. Her purse strap slid forward, getting in her way. The handbag was light, elegant. Rich-looking. They wouldn't know it contained a learner's permit, a bus pass, a student ID, and a tampon. She gulped more water, using her off hand to lift the strap over her head.

When she turned, they were arrayed around her in a semicircle, still not too close but blocking her exits. The smallest ran at her. She threw the purse into his face and pivoted, dashing between the fountain and a dark mass of boys, sprinting diagonally over grass toward the streetlight at the corner. Hearing their voices but not listening, running, turning her ankle, running, crossing the intersection, running, across a parking lot, slowing, panting, sweating, on a well-lit street between a bus stop and a restaurant. She did not look behind her. If they thought her worth chasing, she'd find out soon enough.

The water had helped, but now she limped on both feet, past a block of restaurants, through a miasma of chorizo, chicken-fried steak, hamburgers, garlic, peppers, bread. Though she knew she was holding her head steady, she had the impression that it was wobbling back and forth.

From streetlight to twilight to streetlight, she walked, past the library, past the craft center, past lost tourists and parking meters and dark glass buildings soaring like star-spangled mountains.

Mountains.

She veered at the next skyscraper and tried the door. Locked. Security saw her through the glass and walked toward her, but she moved on, trying the next door, and the next.

The one that opened had a restaurant. The marble floor was cool under her sore feet, the air-conditioning cold on her sweat. She walked past the golden light of the restaurant, into the lobby, where a modern fountain with a push bar permitted her to drink, and drink, and drink, until her stomach sloshed. Elevators would be cheating, but she turned corners until she found the heavy metal door that opened onto the stairs, which were incandescently bright, warm, and concrete.

Her sore ankle and knee faltered, and were soon joined by a matched set of aching calves. At each landing she paused to muster breath for the next climb. Sometimes she climbed with her eyes closed, sometimes she pulled herself hand over hand along the rail. Up, and up, and up. How tall was this building?

Six. Ten. Directly from twelve to fourteen. At eighteen, she heard a door open and voices, echoing unintelligibly through the vacuum of concrete and light, below her. *Slap, thud, slap,* to the nineteenth floor, the twentieth. Blood pounded in her ears and across her forehead and in her chest. Sweat prickled in every private crevice and tickled her upper lip. Her legs screamed in pain. Nausea crept under the membranes of her eyes and into the tender skin inside her elbows. Twenty-one, twenty-two, twenty-three, twenty-four.

R. *R* for "roof." The top of the mountain at last.

The energy of the air-conditioning unit vibrated in her bones and against the soles of her feet, in her palms, as she pressed the bar and pushed open the door. Beyond lay one more flight of stairs, rising into a hollow concrete block that existed solely to conduct her through another metal door. She was so tired she expected it to be locked, but felt no surprise when it swung open. She was in a box perched atop the building, a mini-twenty-first floor—inexplicably built just a little too high, so that instead of stepping directly onto the roof, you had to go down again.

The warm air cooled her sweat before she stepped out onto metal steps, which shook and clanged as she descended to the roof surface. Wind whipped her hair into her mouth, jerked her skirt into her face, and shoved her down to the roof, where the wall that rimmed the building halved the indignity.

The city spread around her, a chaos of intermeshing lights, some stationary, some flowing, some leaping skyward along the lines of the buildings they obscured, some rippling horizontally out from the dark center of herself, sinking to the sticky pebbly surface of the roof. She melted like the Witch of the West, straight down, breathing deep ragged breaths, wondering if she should have held out for the landmark tower that still loomed above her, with its tacky revolving restaurant. Not necessary. This square solid roof was revolving nicely, thank you, and swaying, too, and the only lights now were the sweeping purplish red Lava lamps inside her lids.

Nothing would happen. Nothing could. What could she say to everybody? How would she get home? Stupid, stupid, stupid . . .

She vomited, losing the water first, then bile, which should have been the end of it, but she kept right on, voiding all the labels.

Liz. Lizzie. Elizabeth. Elizabitch. Beth. Betty. Good Girl. Solid A–B student. Yearbook staff. Daughter. Sister. Friend. Niece. Target. Survivor. Benefactor. Churchgoer. Doubter. Liar. Truth teller. Up they came, in no particular order, spreading around her in a disgusting puddle of identity, until she was empty, done, limp, unable to tell whether her eyes were open or shut.

Scrape.

Rustle.

Flap.

Her totem animal was black and hunched, trailing a pale train of feathers at the ends of her wings. She hopped forward, wings spread for balance, and peered into the alien human face.

A vulture? All this way, all that walking, that trail of belongings and identities and risks, and at the end of the day her totem was a *vulture?*

You have a problem with that? the vulture asked.

"Um—no," she said. "It's just that vultures have this reputation."

Reputation is not self, said the vulture. **You don't care about one once you have the other. But if you refuse your self when it's shown to you, I can't help you.**

"All right," she said. "Show me."

The vulture hopped onto her head, claws stabbing her scalp and wings spreading above her like a tent. The world sank away into glaring daylight as she soared, flapped, soared again, wafted upward on a column of warm air.

The city lay below, complete in its complexity. She saw the patterns in its chaos and the chaos in its patterns—the streets that bound it together, the highways that pulled it apart. People had shaped and limited the space, but between, above, below, were cats, dogs, egrets, pigeons, sparrows, skunks, possums, rats, fish, frogs—scores of species, totems all.

A hawk shot past, catching a pigeon on the wing. On the ground, a cat pounced on a grasshopper, a dog rolled in the oily mud outside a garage, a heron stole a crab from the bins behind a seafood restaurant.

You are not predator nor prey, said the vulture, **nor the highest, nor the swiftest; but you see far enough and fight hard enough, when the need is there. You can rise above anything. You can reject that, and remain as you are, or you can embrace it, and daily become more like yourself.**

"Is there a third choice?"

Usually, said the vulture, **but it's up to you to find that.**

She flapped and soared and flapped from one end of the city to the other as the seasons reeled below, fall flickering to winter, winter to spring to endless summer to fall again. For a watchful vulture, opportunity was everywhere, discarded by those who didn't recognize or want it.

"It's lonesome up here."

Is it? Look around.

She saw them—turkey vultures, soaring, and black vultures, like herself, soaring, flapping, soaring, flapping, circling high, scanning the streets and lots and fields, the dumps and roads. Evening came, and the black vultures roosted together; morning came, and they flew off in clusters, straight to the biggest carcasses.

We tend to clump around the best opportunities. You'll have some fights. But so what?

"So what?"

She laughed, soaring higher and higher, until she broke through the cloud cover to the roof of the skyscraper, sore and exhausted and still laughing, barefoot, penniless, with no resources but her bare self to get her home and explain the apparent mess she'd made—but that would be enough.

The vulture hopped back into the shadows as Elizabeth stood, shaky in her limbs, solid at her core.

Ready to start being who she was.

● *by*
Joseph
Bruchac

These days most people don't believe in love at first flight, I mean sight. But I do-oo-oo, and it's killing me. You get this aching feeling in the middle of your stomach, something that won't go away no matter how many mice you eat. Even an entire rabbit—not one of those little guys, but a big snowshoe jobbie—doesn't get rid of it.

Believe me, I tried it and I know. I sat there on my favorite perch hoping that when I coughed up that round, fur-coated pellet studded with crunched-up bunny bones, the pain in my gut (like being impaled on the sharp end of a broken branch) would come up with it, tumble to the ground with a soft thump, and be gone. No such luck. Pellet ejected, pain still present.

And what made it worse was that she walked by just then. She was wearing that same doeskin dress she had on when I first saw her. I've seen her in other clothes. (To be honest, I've also seen her without any clothes. There's this convenient cedar tree that overhangs the place where the long river has swirled out a deep pothole by the dawnside bank. That's her favorite place to bathe in the morning. Whoo-hoo-hooo! Oh my! Yes indeed it is.) But I like best the way she looks in that dress. It is such soft deerskin that it just flows over her figure, making those curves of her body much more interesting to observe.

And the dress only comes down to her knees, so I can see the brown swell of her strong calves and the way her feet are caressed by porcupine-quill-beaded moccasins. Those little toes of hers inside those moccasins (visible, of course, when she takes them off to wade into the stream) are so sweet. Thinking of her perfectly shaped little toes makes me want to nibble on them.

No, I am not talking about eating them. I am not that kind of a creature, one of those dark beings that uses a sweet voice to lure a human off into the depths of the forest.

Yoooo-hoooooo, I not terrible hungry creature with huge mouth and teeth sharper than those of woo-ooolf. I actually gorgeous, sexy, love-starved being just like you but of opposite sex if that is what you pre-fer-er. Just keep on following my voice, a little farrr-therr into my scary ca-ave. Got ya, sucker. Arr-rooolf, burp.

No, I am not one of those. I'm referring to romance, not a midnight snack. Nibbles. Little soft love bites starting at the nape of the neck, working down through the soft feathers, ah, hair, in her case. Singing one of those sweet little owl love songs that thrills your chosen one right down to the pinfeathers. Getting your partner all excited and making those little cooing noises and then . . . Well, you know what I mean.

Naturally, Dojihla didn't see me. Dojihla. Did I mention that is her name? Isn't it a beautiful name? It is almost a song. Dojihla, Dojihla. And it is perfect for her. It means "She goes by." Which is what she does whenever I see her. She just goes by. And what if she had looked up? All she would have seen was an owl. Admittedly, a very large, extremely capable, young male owl. She would surely have taken note of the fact that he was an owl well above average. No way could she miss that special gleam of intelligence in the eyes, the sensitivity of the beak, the way each feather had been so elegantly preened. All right, I know. I'm dreaming.

Nowadays, to be honest, most of the dreaming I do is daydreaming. I'm not sleeping the way I should. I've always been a light sleeper. Ever since I was small, I've had this bad habit of waking up in the middle of the day. Then, instead of sensibly closing my eyes and going back to sleep until it was properly dark out, I would look around. I never understood what I'd been looking around for until I saw her. Then I knew.

Back in the time of the oldest ones, that would not have been so much of a problem. At least if I understand Great-grandmother's stories right. Back then, not long after Changer shaped the land and the various beings came forth, things weren't as . . . stiff. Creation was more easygoing, you might say. Now you have trees and people, stones and birds, fish and animals, and so on. A tree is a tree is a tree. But back then, you could be a tree one moment and a human being the next.

Great-grandmother says it has something to do with being able both to tell the story and understand it. The real story, she says (and when she does this, her voice gets all soft and whootully), is not about shape, but about spirit. Spirit moves in all life and flows through all things. Once you understand that, you understand the real rules. Then, Great-grandmother says, you can just be yourself.

Back then, in the time of the old ones, having a different shape was no barrier for real love. Trees fell in love with rocks, women fell in love with bears, and so on. Then one or the other would change his or her shape so they could be together.

"Although sometimes," Great-grandmother said, "they needed a little help from those who knew how to transform."

When I first heard that story from Great-grandmother, it both excited and confused me. For days after that, I would do weird things. I would land in a tree and look at its trunk and say, "Hey tree, who-hoo-hooo, are you my lovey?" Or I would catch a mouse and hold it up in one claw and sing to it, "Whoo-ho-hoo, want to marry an owl, dude? No-oo-oo? Oh-oh-kay." Gulp.

It began to bug out my parents.

"Wa-wa-wabi," Father would hoot. "Cut that oooooo-ooout."

"Son, kill your foo-oo-ood befo-o-ore you play with it," Mother would whoo-tu-lul.

Soon I started becoming a devoted people watcher. Even though they didn't have feathers, they looked good to me, so good that it made me begin to wonder about my own bloodline. Had one of those owls back then been a human who finally woke up to the fact that life was much better with wings? Back then when it was different?

Nowadays, in these modern times, we have gotten so forgetful that a lot of beings just can't seem to see how deeply connected we all are. Those humans are the worst at forgetting. Or maybe I should say they are the best because they do so much of it. When you can remember as Great-grandmother does, you don't just remember the things that have happened, but the things that are happening now and the things that are going to happen just as well. Is that confusing to you? I hope it is because it confuses the feathers right off me.

"Wa-wa-wa-bi," Great-grandmother whoots, "Think it is bad noooo-ooow? I remember when it is go-oing to be much wooo-oorse."

That's the kind of stuff she is always saying. Thinking about it gives me a pain in my head in addition to the ache in my stomach. So I don't think about it. My problem is not the distant future. It is now. It is Dojihla. Well, actually, it is Dojihla and me.

Keep it simple is what Great-grandmother says. See your problem, then swoop down on it.

Simple? All right. Here it is. How can I get her, Dojihla, to love me, Wabi? Especially when she is so darn picky.

Do I sound like I'm finding fault with the one I love? Unh-hunh, yes. Love may have made me sick to my stomach, but it hasn't made me blind. Graceful as she is, beautiful as she is, perfect as she may be in form and movement, that human girl is just as finicky. I know because I have been watching her so closely—as has every human youth in every village for four days' flight around. They all know who Dojihla is. She is the lovely maiden with the sparkling eyes—and the sarcastic voice—the one whose words are sharper than flint-tipped arrows.

It has gotten to the point where suitors have almost stopped coming around. Most of them have become afraid of what she'll say to any man foolhardy enough to seek her hand. With a few well-aimed words or a single gesture, she can destroy the tallest, strongest, most capable suitor. However, there always seems to be at least one who thinks he can succeed where others fail.

Today it was Bezo, who came all the way from the village by the rapids. Bezo had made up a special song for her, a song that he was certain had such power no woman could resist it. It spoke of her beauty, her grace, her sweetness (oops!), comparing her to flowers, swaying reeds, and a doe with her fawn.

Dojihla's parents looked over anxiously at their daughter when Bezo finished singing. Both her father and her mother have been eager for her to find a husband. They had hopes that this young man would be the one. Bezo was known to be a good hunter, and that is one of the primary duties a son-in-law owes to his new family.

I watched anxiously from my perch in a nearby pine. It hadn't been that good a song. And Bezo's voice was not the best. Also I would have chosen to compare her with a mountain lion rather than that wimpy mama deer. But maybe *I* was being picky. Music has always been one of my special gifts. My parents have always said that I have one of the best voices. However, I wasn't sure that a human could appreciate owl singing.

Dojihla looked up; her eyes seemed faraway, as if entranced by that song. Bezo leaned forward, eager to hear her declaration of love.

"What *was* that?" Dojihla said. "Did I just hear a moose farting?"

I almost fell off my branch with laughter. For his part, Bezo went pale, stood up, turned, and stalked off.

Dojihla's mother looked up into my tree. "My husband, what is wrong with that owl?" she said. "It sounds as if it is choking."

"Forget the bird, my wife," said Dojihla's father.

There was a look in his eyes that told me what had happened was like that last stick pulled from the beaver dam, the one that makes the pent-up water come rushing forth.

"We must talk."

Then the two of them went into their lodge, where their daughter could not hear them.

Of course I could. If you can hear the deliciously terrified heartbeat of a mouse hiding in the grass far below your treetop perch, it is not at all difficult to make out a human conversation within a nearby wigwam. That conversation! It both worried me and gave me hope.

"Our daughter now has lived for seventeen winters," Dojihla's father whispered. "It is past time for her to choose a husband."

"But how can we find any man who is stupid, I mean *suitable* enough?" said Dojihla's mother. "Our daughter is so choosy."

"My wife," Dojihla's father replied. "We shall no longer allow her to choose. We will have a contest. The man who brings in the most game in a day will be the winner. We will tell our daughter that she cannot refuse such a man."

I took flight from the tree while they were still talking. Whoo-hoo, hooo! I knew what I had to do. I was certain Great-grandmother would help me.

"Wa-wa-wa-bi," Great-grandmother said, "don't you think it would be better for this human girl to love you for your real self? Don't you think she could love the bravest and strongest of all the owls in the forest? The owl who is so generous he would share his last mouse with a friend?"

I shook my head so hard that I loosened a few feathers. "No-oo-ooo!"

Great-grandmother was silent for a while. Then she made one of those soft little whoot-a-luls that is an owl's way of sighing. "So-oo-ooo, you are sure this is what you wa-ant, Wa-wa-wa-bi?"

"Yes."

I could have said more, but I kept it at that. Knowing Great-grandmother—whose favorite saying was *Those who know the most say the least*—a short answer was always better.

Great-grandmother turned her head one way and then the next, moving her gaze through the circle of creation surrounding us. Then she took flight. At her age, that was unusual. She relied more on food that was brought to her than on her own hunting. To be honest, I had actually thought she no longer was able to fly, and that had worried me at times, knowing what would happen if a flock of crows should ever spy out the hiding place she had chosen within the lightning-blasted trunk of an ancient oak, and then dive in to attack her.

But Great-grandmother's flight was strong and certain.

"Whooo," she said as she circled me the first time.

"Whooo," she repeated as she came around me the second time. I had to keep turning my head to watch her as she flew. I couldn't help it.

"WHOOOOO," she called yet again, flying around me a third time, so fast that I found myself becoming dizzy.

"WHOOO ARE YOOOUUUU?" she hooted so loudly that it almost deafened me as she made a fourth and final tighter circle that ended with her not going around me but flying right at me!

Thoomph! Her right wing struck me in the chest. She didn't hit me hard, but I lost my balance and felt myself falling backward. I tried to open my own wings to catch the wind, but something was wrong. My feathers weren't spreading out as they should. Then, all of a sudden—WHOMP!—I landed on my back at the base of the tree. I wasn't hurt because the moss was thick there, but it took the wind out of me, and I didn't feel like moving for a while.

Things looked different. I could see the light of the day in a different way. I didn't feel hurt, but when I turned my head, my neck felt unusually tight. I raised my arm to feel my beak and was shocked at how soft it was, and what were these even softer things under it and around my mouth? Lips. I had lips. For that matter, what were these wiggly worms at the ends of my wings? Fingers? I sat up and looked at myself. I was a human being.

Great-grandmother landed on a low branch next to me.

"We-elll," she said.

I remembered my manners. "Ktsi wliwini," I said. "Great thanks to you, Great-grandmother. But . . ."

I paused. It wasn't because I didn't know what to say, but because I didn't know which to say of the many things that swarmed through my head like bees. I was also fascinated with this new body I found myself in. There were so many things that were . . . different.

"Yoo-oou have questions," Great-grandmother said. "But first, Wa-wa-wa-bi, if you are to be a hu-uu-man, do-ooo not play with that part of yoo-oo-urself in public."

I looked back up at her and smiled. It was the first time I had ever smiled, and it felt quite pleasant, almost as pleasant as . . .

"Wa-wa-wa-biiiii," Great-grandmother said.

"I hear you, Great-grandmother," I said, holding up my hands. "But what shall I do now? I have no clothing, and humans always wear clothing. I also do not have human weapons to hunt with, and I—" I stopped, realizing that I was talking far too much. Apparently finding it hard to keep your beak shut was also part of being a human being.

Great-grandmother nodded her head and lifted up one foot to point with a long talon at a hollow in the base of her tree.

I stood up and walked—human legs were longer than I had realized, but I got the knack of it quickly—over to that hollow and reached inside. My hands proved as good at grasping as my feet had been when I was in the shape of an owl. I pried out a long bundle wrapped in an old deerskin and tied tightly with rawhide. Those new fingers of mine were clever enough to know what to do on their own as they untied that string and unwrapped the bundle.

"Ho-ho-hoooo," I said in pleasure at what I saw. There were all the clothes a human man would wear, from the fringed shirt and breechcloth down to moccasins that were, I was pleased to see, decorated with porcupine-quill patterns much like those on Dojihla's shoes. Not only that, there was a fine bow with its double-twisted string wrapped about it, a quiver of arrows, and a flint knife inside a leather sheath that could be hung around my neck.

It was a bit awkward, but with Great-grandmother's hooted instructions to help me, I got the clothing on. Then I held out my arms and looked at her.

Great-grandmother nodded. But there was a look in her eyes as she did so that made me step closer to her. She turned her head away from me.

"These were my great-grandfather's," I said. "He was a human who changed?" I spoke it as a question, but there was no doubt in my mind. I knew and understood more than I ever had understood before.

"He was a gooo-ooo-ood hunter," Great-grandmother hooted in a voice that was both sad and proud. "Whoo-hoo-ever he was, I loved him for himself. But I will not tell you his stoo-oo-ory to-oo-day. It is yoo-our time, Great-grandson."

"I have more questions, more things I must know. Will I always stay a human now? Can I ever change back into an owl again?" I said. Strange how speaking with human lips made words flow so quickly. Strangest of all, I didn't even feel like hooting when I talked.

Great-grandmother looked amused. 'Yo-oo-oou are who-oo-oo you-oo-oo are," she said. "It will be yo-oour cho-o-ice, Great-grandson. Who-oo-oo you-oo-oou really are will never change. Feel you-oo-our ears."

I reached up my hands to my ears. To my surprise, they were long on top and stiff. They stuck up out of my long black hair just as the two tufts of feathers on top of my head had done when I was an owl.

"Oh, no-oo-oo," I moaned. "Now anyone who sees me will kno-ooow."

Great-grandmother looked amused. But she said nothing.

"Great-grandmother," I pleaded, "this is serious. I have to hide these."

"Are you-oo-oo sure you-oo-oo want to co-o-ver those lo-o-vely ears?"

"Yes," I said. "I am very sure. Tell me what I can do."

Great-grandmother did not reply. Instead she just lifted up her foot again and pointed with her claw at the leather headband that still remained on the ground. I had seen such things worn by the men of Dojihla's village. I understood. I picked the leather up and wrapped it tightly so that my owl's ears were pressed down and concealed by the headband.

"No-oo-ooww," Great-grandmother hooted. "Goo-oo-oo hunt."

I'd never hunted in the daylight before. Things look different than at night. You can see your prey from so much farther away—and it can see you. That all took some getting used to. For some reason, learning to use the bow and arrows wasn't difficult. I tried doing what I had seen some of the young boys do. You know that training game. You make a ball of sticks, tie it together with basswood bark, and then throw it up high in the air. The idea is to try to nock an arrow to your string and then shoot it at that ball before it hits the ground. Not only did I get an arrow off on the first try, I hit that fist-size ball of sticks dead center.

"Whoo-hoo-hooo," I yelled in excitement. Then I thought about what I had just yelled. Hmmm.

The next hard part about hunting was remembering what to hunt. I had just crept close enough to the most delicious-looking chipmunk to take a shot when it came to me that humans liked bigger food. Forget about mice, shrews (which have a nice sharp tang to them), baby crows (yummy and crunchy). Think big. Even bigger than bunnies. Deer. Elk. Moose. Got it.

And I got them. Stealth came easily to me after I learned to approach them with the wind in my face. And my arrows struck just where I wanted them to strike. Those big animals were a little difficult to move, but luckily this new body of mine was strong.

That evening, as the last light was disappearing in the sunrise direction, I walked into Dojihla's village. Everyone was gathered around a big fire. Several other young men were there ahead of me, each with the game they had killed piled in front of them. They ranged from a big young man who had two deer and a beaver to one poor loser who had nothing at his feet but a scrawny woodchuck.

Dojihla was eyeing all of them with equal displeasure. But when I stepped into the firelight and she looked at me, I thought I saw a different expression on her face. I read it as *This is too good to be true.*

That pleased me even more than the realization that I was at least a hand's width taller than the biggest of the other young men who sought her as their wife—the nervous-looking fat-faced one whom Dojihla's father had been about to announce as the winner.

"I have come for the contest," I said. And I said it just that way. No long-drawn-out Os at all. I'd been practicing.

Then I dropped the two big bucks I'd been carrying, one over each shoulder. They were both larger than the two Fat Face had brought.

"Two deer," Dojihla's father said.

"Plump ones," said her mother with a big smile.

Dojihla said nothing.

Oops, I thought. Not a good sign. But I refused to let worry get in my way—or Fat Face, who was now being poked in the back by an older woman.

"Speak up, son," she commanded.

"I, ah, I have two deer AND a beaver," Fat Face said in a surprisingly unenthusiastic voice.

I raised my hand. "Wait," I said.

Then I walked back out of the firelight to return with an elk over my shoulders. I placed it next to the two deer, noticed the look on people's faces, and decided that carrying a full-grown elk may have been a little too impressive. So next time I just dragged in the bull moose by its antlers. When I straightened up, I saw that everyone—except for Dojihla—appeared to be trying to catch flies with their mouths.

Dojihla's father was the first to recover. "This young man has won," he said, placing a hand on my shoulder.

"He will be my son-in-law," Dojihla's mother said, wrapping her arms around me.

Once again, Dojihla had nothing to say. Her eyes were not looking at me, but through me. I felt a little shiver of uncertainty go down my spine, like when you have absentmindedly fallen asleep on a branch and wake up to what may have been the sound of a crow calling its mates. Uh-oh.

But things went well at first. The other young men came over to congratulate me. They didn't look disappointed. They had all been pushed into the competition by their parents, who were eager for the prestige to be gained by their son marrying the chief's daughter. Even Fat Face seemed relieved that he had not won Dojihla. I wondered if the woodchuck killer might have been a better hunter than I thought.

"She is yours," Fat Face said, grasping my forearm with his right hand in a way that led me to quickly grasp his the same way. "May you survive it."

Then preparations began for the feast. They sat me down in front of the fire with Dojihla by my side. They had cut meat from the animals I brought in, and soon the chunks were cooking over the fire, and they smelled good.

Smell. That was a new thing to me. I had known little of that in my old shape. I began to appreciate more why humans have noses. This smelling was a good thing. I looked over at Dojihla. Her nose was the most pleasing to look at of all the young women there. I smiled at her, and she smiled back sweetly.

Too sweetly. I began to realize that I had been concentrating too much on all these pleasant new sensations. Smelling with my nose. Touching everything with my fingers, feeling my lips with my tongue, tugging now and then at the hair that hung down past my chin. I'd never had a chin before. Or long legs and knees that bend forward. Strange. And it was so hard to pick things up now with those short toes, even when I took off my new moccasins. It was like being in a dream.

"Husband-to-be," a voice whispered close to my ear. Warm breath caressed my cheek. I turned to look into Dojihla's eyes, and what I saw was not the sweetness in her voice. There was a challenge and a question, there was suspicion and stubbornness. And I knew two things. The first was that I was in trouble. The second was that I had no idea how to get out of it.

"Yes," I answered. *Say the least,* I thought.

Dojihla reached up a hand to touch my face. "You are feeling too hot?" she asked in an innocent tone that made a chill go down my back. How could I not be feeling hot with all of the logs she had been piling onto the fire next to us?

"You are very warm," she continued. One of her fingers brushed something wet from my forehead.

Warm *and* wet? I put one hand up to feel it. It was true. Moisture was leaking out of my skin. Was something wrong with me? I held my wet hand out by the fire. It wasn't blood.

"You are sweating so much," Dojihla said. "I am sure your headband is too hot."

"Yes," I agreed.

This time, as you have probably already guessed, saying the least was not the best. But I was confused. After all, I'd only been a human for half the span of a day. When owls are hot, they don't sweat. They just pant or fan their wings.

"Then let us take that headband off," Dojihla said, reaching up both her hands.

"Yes," I said, then: "No-oo-ooo."

But it was too late. Quicker than a bat snatching a moth out of the air, Dojihla whipped that leather band from around my head, and my two tall owl ears popped up.

Dojihla stood and stepped back. Triumph gleamed in her bright eyes.

"Look," she shouted, pointing at me as she did so. "I promised I would marry the man who was the best hunter. But this one is not a man. See those ears. This one is not a human being. Perhaps he was planning to devour me as soon as he got me alone."

My heart was breaking. I stood, looked around the circle of firelight at the shocked faces staring at me, and shook my head. "No-ooo-ooo," I said. "No-oo-ooo."

But that was all I could think to say, and I knew as soon as I said it how I sounded. Not like a man at all. I turned away and walked into the darkness.

I do not know how long I walked. I was confused. Part of the confusion was from the pain that now filled the very center of my being. Admittedly, another part was from the pain in my forehead I'd gotten by walking head-on into a large maple tree soon after I stalked out into the darkness. Not only had it spoiled the wounded dignity of my exit (the *ka-bonk-Ouch!* had to have been audible to all those I left behind), it reminded me that I no longer had the night vision of an owl.

I wanted to find my way back to Great-grandmother's tree, but I couldn't. I didn't know where I was. Nothing was familiar to me here in the lower darkness beneath the canopy of branches that had been my home territory. Finally, my new legs refused to move any farther and I allowed them to collapse beneath me and I slept. I slept all through that day and on into the night.

When I opened my eyes again, the gentle touch of darkness was around me. And I heard a soft voice.

"Whoo-hoo-hoo," it trilled. "Great-grandson."

I squinted my eyes and looked around. The moon began to shine just then through the trees. I could see enough to make out the shape of my great-grandmother on a branch next to me. Somehow I had found my way to her tree, which I now realized was rising above me. I had slept on the same bed of moss where I'd first stretched out my new fingers.

"Great-grandmother," I said. "I have lost her."

"Wa-wa-wa-bi," Great-grandmother said. She leaned close to me to gently nibble my earlobe. Then she began to run her beak through my tangled hair. I closed my eyes, remembering what it was like when I was a little owlet and my mother preened my feathers in just this way. It didn't take away the pain that had settled like a too-big stone in my crop, but it did make me feel calmer. I lifted up my hand to wipe my face. For some reason, even though the night was cool, I was sweating now from my eyes.

I looked at my great-grandmother. I had no idea how old she was, how many winters she had lived through, or how many more she would survive. But I knew that it was said among the Owl People that she was even older than the giant oak in which she made her roost. I was certain there could be no one who knew more, no being who had gained more wisdom in her long, long life. And I realized what question I needed to ask her.

"What did I do wrong?" I asked.

Great-grandmother clicked her beak in pleasure. "Goo-oo-ood questio-on, Great-grandson. Wha-at do-oo yo-ou think yo-ou did?"

So I told her. When I finished, Great-grandmother clicked her beak again.

"Wa-wa-wa-bi," she said. "Yo-ou cannot win someone's lo-ove by fo-oo-ooling them. I to-old yo-ou that yo-ou must be who-oo-oo yo-ou are."

"But who-oo—I mean who am I? Am I a human being or an owl, or am I an owl pretending to be a human, or am I only half a human being who can never be an owl again, or—" I stopped. It seemed that I was a little too human when it came to talking too much.

Great-grandmother nodded her head. "Yo-ou are Wa-wa-wa-bi," she said.

Then she lifted up her foot and pointed with her claw at that same hole in the base of the tree where I had found the bundle that held my clothing and hunting gear. I went over to it, knelt down, and reached inside, farther than I had reached before. This time my fingertips found a smaller bundle and pulled it out. It felt as if there was a stick wrapped within it. But when I untied the bundle, I saw it was like no stick I had ever seen before. It had been hollowed out, and there were holes in it.

Without my telling them to do so, my fingers lifted that hollow stick up to my mouth. As soon as my lips touched it, I found myself compelled to blow into it. Whooo-heee-hooo. A delicate bird-note came out of that stick. It was almost like the sweet singing I had done when I was an owl.

"It is a fluu-uu-ute, Wa-wa-wa-bi," Great-grandmother whoo-tled to me.

And I understood. That was how my great-grandmother's heart had been won long ago. This flute had been made and played by my human great-grandfather. Its music had shown her what he held in his heart. I knew what I had to do. I had to learn to play this flu-uu-ute—no, flute. I had to make up a song of my own that would tell Dojihla who I was—not an inhuman being, but one whose love had changed him forever.

I practiced and listened, practiced and listened more. The notes began to run together the way the waters of a stream flow over the stones and ripple down into the wide calm of the lake. I put moonlight and sunset into my song, added the wind beneath my lost wings and the touch of the sun on my face at dawn, the trem-ble of my breath when I first saw her face, the yearning for her to look my way, the hope I felt when I thought I'd won her, even the pain of having lost my chance when she saw through my decep-tion. Most of all, I put into it who I was. Wabi. Just Wabi.

I practiced where I thought I could not be heard, but I did not stay away from her village. I came each day to watch her from among the trees as she went about her work. Much of her time was spent scraping the hides of a moose, an elk, and two deer that were tied to tanning racks outside the wigwam she shared with her parents. I noticed how she seemed to look now and then toward the edge of the village, toward that place where I had walked off into the night. I also noticed how she took her water jug along the path that led to the spring.

Finally, even though it was not perfect and never would be, I thought my song was good enough. I had chosen the spot carefully. It was a fallen pine that lay next to the spring trail, just after the first sharp bend around the hill. It was in plain sight to anyone who chose to come around that bend after hearing the sound of a flute.

It was not long after dawn. The sun was only two fingers above the horizon when I saw Dojihla leave her wigwam carrying an empty water pot. I made my way quickly to the fallen pine by a shortcut I had chosen. Then I sat, listening. My big ears were uncovered. No headband this time. So I could clearly hear her feet on the trail, despite the fact that she had not yet reached the bend. It was hard to catch my breath, even though I had not run a long way. But I had to try. My fingers felt awkward, and the first note came out all wrong, almost like the squawk of a jay.

But I couldn't stop. I closed my eyes and kept playing. *I am Wabi*, I thought. *This is my song. This is me.*

And as I played, the music began to sing itself. The flute became both my throat and the throat of the wind, my song and the sweetest melodies of the birds. It was owl song, sunset and sunrise, my heart and hers beating together, my breath and hers breathing out and breathing in. I reached the last note and held it as long as I could, trilling it until my breath gave out and I had to stop.

Then I opened my eyes and looked. There was no one in front of me. A sob started to come from my throat, but it was stopped by the hand that touched my shoulder. I turned to find Dojihla sitting next to me on the log.

"Who are you?" she said.

"I am Wabi," I said.

"Unh-hunh," she answered, her eyes holding mine. There was no doubt in her eyes this time. She reached both her hands up to stroke my ears. "I am Dojihla."

● *by*
Terry
Trueman

HONESTLY, TRUTHFULLY

This morning I've decided to make myself over—easy, huh?

Honestly, truthfully, I guess the answer depends on what you mean by *makeover*. I'm thinking about all those dumb-ass "reality" TV shows about totally remodeling people's houses for them when they're gone for fifteen minutes, or about getting liposuctioned and butox-injected and going from looking like a regular, kind of homely, fat person to looking like a not regular, less homely, skinny person. You know the shows I mean: nerd to stud, wallflower to runway model, dipshit to cool guy.

Well, I don't have the money or time or energy for that level of makeover, so mine is gonna be a lot simpler and more straightforward—I'm gonna go from being a liar to being . . . well . . . NOT a liar.

Today I'm going to tell people the truth—like they say on Court TV shows, "the whole truth and nothing but the truth." All my life I've been afraid to do it, but today I'm going to. And here's why—yesterday I noticed that *nobody tells the truth.*

What happened was, I heard this checkout guy at Wal-Mart say to this customer, "So how are you today, sir?" and the customer said, "Great, really, fantastic, how 'bout yerself?" and the check-out guy said, "Absolutely wonderful."

I was the next guy in line, standing right behind the "great, really fantastic" customer guy. I looked up at the two of them. I stared at their faces and at their mouths as they were talking. I watched their eyes and I realized, I just absolutely *knew,* that they were *completely, 100 percent lying!* How did I know? Well, you've heard that expression "It takes one to know one"? When it comes to lying, I am a sixth-degree black belt with whipped cream and a cherry the size of Rhode Island on top. I think that's called a mixed metaphor or a dangling modifier—something like that, I'm not sure. See, I'm already telling the truth! This is easy!

The checkout guy and the customer at Wal-Mart were not all that happy. I know for sure that they weren't having as great a day as they claimed; otherwise they wouldn't have been able to completely click off their happy-go-lucky attitudes in the first millionth of a nanosecond after they were finished talking.

So I said to the checkout guy, when it was my turn, "Are you really having that swell of a day?"

"You betcha!" he answered, and smiled real big.

"Bullshit!" I said. It just kinda slipped outta me.

"I beg your pardon?" His big toothy smile was all gone.

"You heard me," I answered, actually kind of nervous.

Then he smiled again. "Have a nice day, sir, and thanks for shopping at Wal-Mart!"

I smiled, too.

And thus the idea of my honesty makeover was born.

I've thought a lot about this, and I've broken down and ana-lyzed lying to become more expert at my truth-telling makeover.

There are three main types of lying: confabulation, where you just make shit up (*I was late because this flying saucer snatched me up and did a bunch of experiments on my wiener*); denial (*You're accusing me of playing with myself in the shower just 'cause I was in the bathroom for an hour and a half? . . . How dare you make such an accusation. . . . You don't have any hidden video cameras in there, do you?*); and omission (*Gloria's hair looks like shit today, she's a good friend, I'm sure she'd want to know and forgive me for telling her. . . .*) Think about how many times, on an average day, you lie. Come on; if you count all three types of lying, I'll bet you can't even begin to add it all up.

So today's the day. From now on, it's truth time for me—total truth. I'm not gonna ask anybody "How you doing?" if I don't care how they're doing; I'm not gonna answer anybody who asks me how I'm doing by saying something like, "Real good, thanks," if I'm not doing real good. No bullshit today, nothing but the truth. For just one day in the life of a master liar, I'm gonna be honest.

It's first period; Mr. Donaldson's human-sexuality class, where we're studying sexual reproduction—duh, huh? I mean the class is called human sexuality. I'm thinkin' that only amoebas and germs and worms and flowers with parts like pistils and flagella and stuff like that can do *asexual* reproduction, although to be totally honest, sometimes when I'm in the shower, I catch a glimpse of how to have sex all by yourself—hey, honesty all day, right?

So anyway, there's this big drawing of the female reproductive organs on a flip chart up front. All the parts. Nobody I know calls it all the "female reproductive organs," but that's what Mr.

Donaldson is calling it—quite a waste of syllables, you know?

I throw my hand up, and Mr. D nods at me. "Yes, do you have a question?"

"Yeah I was wondering why you didn't use a more normal word for some of the female reproductive organs—you know, something like *pooty,* or maybe a term like—"

Mr. D interrupts me. "Are you out of your goddamned mind?"

I don't think he means to swear. It just flies out of him . . . you know, like an *honest* reaction.

Now normally, seeing a teacher get all red-faced and hearing him swear at me would send me into a fit of confabulation— something like, "Jeez, Mr. D, sorry, but I bumped my head this morning and landed face-first in a huge pile of paint chips, and I've been kinda dizzy and fulla crap ever since." But not today— today I give him several examples of the words I think he oughta be using. . . .

I'm sitting with Mr. Myers, the vice principal in charge of discipline. I realize that I'm kind of lying to Mr. Myers by omission right this very second. He has red hair, the really bright kind that they use, colorwise, for stoplights. I want to ask him whether cars ever slam on their brakes when he stands on a street corner. I can't get a word in edgewise, though; he's yelling too loudly.

He bellows, "Are you trying to get kicked out of school?"

"Nope. I just—"

"Shut up!" Mr. Myers snaps.

I really want to ask him about the red-hair thing, but before I can do it, he throws me out of his office.

I realize that I've lied by omission. I shoulda asked him about his hair. I'm kinda mad at myself. I'm back out in the hallway and "on probation," as Mr. Myers put it.

But now I see Brenda Allenby walking toward me.

Brenda's a popular girl—a cheerleader and one of those happy people who is always smiling at everybody all the time. She's wearing the tightest, cutest little pink T-shirt I've ever seen.

"Hi, Kyle," she says as she walks toward me.

"Hi, Brenda," I answer, then, just keeping it real, and still totally pissed at myself for not asking Mr. Myers the question I wanted to ask him, I add, "Your breasts certainly look perky today—have I ever told you about how often I think about you during my rather extended shower rituals?"

Whew!! There!!! No lies of omission in that question!!!

Brenda's mouth drops open in total shock.

I quickly add, "Nice tongue!"

Brenda's been dating Alex Baldwin, (no relation to the famous actor guy named Alex or Alec or whatever it is Baldwin—except that they are both VERY big, strong-looking guys).

I don't even notice that Alex (the one Brenda's dating) is standing right behind me when I make my honest remarks to her.

Now I realize it.

Alex asks me, "What did you just say to her?"

I realize that what I'd normally do in this situation is try denial: "What is it that you think you heard me say, Alex? You probably thought I said 'perky breasts,' didn't you? No, not at all. What I said was 'jerky pests.' You know, jerks, pests . . ." Okay, admittedly that probably wouldn't work anyway, but before today, denial in some form or another would have been my first reaction. But I'm doing my makeover, and so I have to be honest.

I ask, "You know what, Alex?"

"What's that?"

"I know you think you're popular because you're a first-string jock guy, but here's the deal: People are only nice to you because you're so huge—nobody really likes you. Sorry to have to tell you this. . . ." I hesitate a moment and realize what I've just said, that little phony apology part at the end. So I add, "Actually, truthfully, I'm not sorry at all."

Alex is smiling slightly. "Jeez, Kyle, thanks so much for your honesty."

A little surprised at how well he's taking this, I answer, "No problem."

Alex adds, "And that thing you said about Brenda's breasts being . . . what was it you said?"

"Perky," I answer. "Wouldn't you agree, Alex?"

"Oh, yeah." Alex smiles more broadly. "I absolutely agree. There's just one more thing, Kyle. . . ."

"Oh?" I ask, thinking to myself that this honesty thing is really going well!

"Ohhh, yeahhhh!" Alex says, kind of slowly, still smiling as he steps closer to me. . . .

It's 11:04 in the morning. The doc says I can't go home until after I take a piss, and that the medicine for the pain might make me a little bit dizzy, so I've gotta wait for a ride from my dad. The doc also says that my ribs should heal up within a few weeks and that we won't know for sure how bad my nose is until the swelling goes down.

It's all okay, though. I mean, I've got time to heal because I've been suspended from school for at least three days anyway; I say "at least three days" because there's gonna be a Student Court hearing to consider further "consequences." I don't know whether I'll be allowed to serve any additional punishments concurrently with my present suspension or not, but it hurts to even breathe (my ribs), and it hurts to be awake (my nose)—so the days away from school will be fine by me.

I think tomorrow I'm gonna try a different makeover experiment; in fact, I might even start today. For a while I thought about calling it my "white-lie" makeover—you know, where you never tell anybody anything but white lies. The whole white-lies thing makes a lot of sense to me right now. I mean, this isn't a real tough call: broken ribs and a broken nose and suspension from school, yep, white lies sound like a pretty good idea!

But it might be a bit too much of a shock to my system after my admittedly failed experiment in total honesty.

I have to think of something else. . . .

Have you ever wondered what would happen if you just didn't say anything but senseless babble to everybody who spoke to you? I mean, what if all you said for a whole day to anybody was some nonsense word like . . . oh, let's say . . . *skungy?*

What if you had a "Skungy Day," where if somebody said "Hi," you just smiled and answered "Skungy"? What if when your math teacher explained an algebraic formula and he asked you if you got it, instead of telling the whole truth and nothing but the truth and answering "Hell, no!" or white-lying and saying, "Oh, yeah, it's pretty clear"—what if you just answered, "Skungy, skungy skungy skungy"?

Uh-oh, here's my dad to pick me up.

"Jeez, Kyle, what happened?"

"Skungy."

"I beg your pardon?"

"Skungy-skungy."

"Hey Doc, what's wrong with my kid?"

"Well, he has some badly bruised ribs and his nose appears to be broken. He seems—"

"No, Doc, what's with the 'skungy' deal?"

"Whaddya mean?"

"Kyle, tell him. . . ."

"Skungy, skungy skungy. Skungy skungy-skungy, skungy."

Both the doc and my dad stare at me, but, skungy, can't say anything but skungy 'cause today's gonna be my skungy day . . . where skungy, and only skungy rules: you know, like "Our Skungy who art in skungy, skungy be thy skungy" . . . or "I pledge askungy to the skungy of the United Skungy of Skungy, and to the skungy for which it skungies. . . ."

Yep it's my Skungy Day all right . . . not just in what Skungy says but in my skungy thoughts, too.

Honestly, really—TRUTHFULLY!!!!

I mean . . .

Skungy, skungy—SKUNGY!!!!

● *by*
Jess
Mowry

THE
RESURRECTION

It had been raining for several days, the kind of dreary, drenching rain that finds every leak in rotten old roofs, traps careless rats in flooded basements, and drowns the small and helpless. The time was only around five o'clock, but the clouds hung low in the late March sky, and it seemed as dark as midnight.

The old bus's ceiling lights were dead, and its ailing heater just fogged up the windows while actually chilling the air. The driver wore gloves and a black hooded parka, a faceless shadow barely seen in the dim greenish glow of the instrument lamps.

Corey was the last soul aboard as the bus rumbled over some railroad tracks to splash its way through narrow streets, past rows of decaying Victorian houses, truck garages, container yards, and rusty piles of jagged junk, its wipers slapping monotonously while the rain rattled down on its roof.

Corey was thirteen and deep, dusky black. He was soaking wet from his walk from school and a half-hour wait at the unsheltered stop. His bushy Afro was coldly dripping, his old sagger jeans felt as heavy as lead, and his big battered sneaks were like water-filled coffins that leaked little rivers across the floor. His ragged puff-coat, a childhood relic, couldn't be zipped above his chest, where his sodden white T-shirt was clinging like paint.

"Coal Street," murmured the driver, bringing the bus to a hissing halt that sent a wave of gutter water rushing over the sidewalk. But he turned to smile at Corey, his face still hidden beneath his hood revealing nothing but shadows and teeth. "Y'all hurry home, son, you'll catch your death."

"Or maybe somebody else's," said Corey, his sneakers making squishy sounds as he shouldered his pack and descended the steps to pause at the edge of a murky stream. "What you got for me today?"

The driver glanced out at the gloomy evening. "It's always darkest before the dawn."

"An' then you put your black shades on. See you tomorrow, Louis."

Mist was creeping in from the bay through the swirling shroud of falling rain, and the feeble streetlights were ringed with gold. The gutter drains were choked with trash, and Corey splashed through oily lakes of swampy-smelling water. Like many West Oakland neighborhoods, his was mostly Victorian houses that looked like miniature haunted mansions, each with a scraggly patch of yard and some with gap-toothed fences. Corey's house was three stories tall and higher than it was wide. It seemed to lean over the sidewalk a little, especially at night, and looked about ready to topple right now as Corey climbed the creaky steps to its high and unlit porch.

"Yo," said a husky voice in the dark.

Corey tensed for fight or flight, expecting a crackhead or some sort of zombie sheltering there from the rain. His hand shot down for his box-cutter blade, but then he relaxed as a small, slim shape materialized out of the shadows. "S'up, Sniffles?" he asked.

"I'm cold. Can I come in?"

Corey smiled at the younger boy, who was almost eleven, as black as himself, and as lean as a coyote he'd seen on TV. The kid was clad in ragged jeans that puddled over his worn-out sneaks and dragged behind on the ground. He was shirtless beneath an army jacket of sandy desert camouflage, a veteran of an endless war, that nearly reached his feet. Its sleeves hung down cartoonishly to well below his knees, while a tattered Oakland Raiders cap adorned his nappy hair.

"Sure, dawg," said Corey. He heard an eerie chattering and realized it was Sniffles's teeth. "Damn, Sniff, you're wetter than me! You wanna catch your death, fool?"

"I'm hungry," said Sniffles, as if that explained everything.

Corey lifted the bill of Sniffles's cap to see at least a part of his face. "Let's go dig somethin' up."

"P-pizza, m-maybe?"

"Dream on, little man, as long as you can." Corey pulled out a big brass skeleton key that hung around his neck on a shoelace and unlocked the house's front door. The hinges made a spooky sound as Corey pushed the door open, revealing a foyer dimly lit by a twenty-watt bulb on the ceiling. The house contained three apartments, but no one seemed to be home right now, and the only sound was the rustle of rain. The boys ascended a squeaky staircase, dripping trails of water, their breaths puffing ghostly smoke in the air, to reach the third-floor landing. The bulb was out in the hallway again, and Corey groped his way to his door with the smaller boy clutching his hand.

"I'm scared of the dark," whispered Sniffles, as if afraid of awakening something. He clung to Corey, squeezing his coat, which spattered the floor like a soggy sponge.

Corey felt for the lock and inserted his key. "You keep runnin' around all wet in the rain, you better get used to the dark, man, 'cause there's no light where it's always night."

"What you sayin'?" demanded Sniffles.

"Nothin', dawg. Bad joke. Forget it."

A streetlamp's glow through the living-room window cast rippling patterns across the floor as rain poured off the house's eaves to rattle the lids of garbage cans and drum on a Dumpster below. Corey let Sniffles enter first, then pushed a switch on the wall. A gold-shaded lamp came on by a couch that was slowly bleeding cotton. Rainwater dripped from the lofty ceiling, plunking into pots and pans all close to overflowing. Corey locked the door, wiggled out of his pack, then went to light the little gas fire that crouched on clawed feet in a corner. He shed his coat and peeled off his shirt, revealing more muscles than actual mass, his chest jutting out like a small pair of bricks, his biceps round as river rocks, while his stomach seemed armored by ebony stone. Even his V-jawed face looked hard, with a wide but snubby bridgeless nose and cheekbones high and fierce.

"Get out them wet clothes," he said to the smaller, shivering boy. "I'ma get somethin' to dry you off."

Sniffles sat bare by the hissing flames, his knees drawn up to his tight little chest and his hair dripping glittering jewels on the floor, as Corey returned with a blanket and towel. "Stand up, little guy, let's get you dry. . . . Damn, you smell like a wet puppy dog."

"Is that bad?" chattered Sniffles as Corey went to work with the towel.

"Probably not to another dog, but a hot bath wouldn't kill you."

"Later, okay? I'm hungry now."

"I'll check what's in the kitchen. But it probably won't be pizza." Corey gave Sniffles the blanket. "Wrap yourself up an' go in the bathroom. You know how to work the water?"

"'Course. We used to have a tub."

"Then fill it up an' get your ass in."

"Aight."

The apartment was starting to warm up a little as Corey got out of his wet shoes and socks, stripped off his jeans, peeled off his boxers, then emptied the brimming pots and pans by dumping them out the window. He went to the tiny kitchen, lit the stove to make coffee, then checked the contents of the wheezy old fridge: half a bowl of mac-and-cheese, a garden salad from Safeway, and most of a gallon jug of milk.

Sniffles appeared in the doorway, robed like a miniature monk in the blanket. "No pizza, huh?"

"Pizza lives in a land faraway, little man, where chocolate cats eat marshmallow rats an' all the happy kids are fat."

Sniffles giggled as if Corey had drawn him a funny picture. "Where's your dad?"

"Workin' the graveyard again. They do most of the diggin' at night anyway so it don't freak out the visitors. If we're lucky, we'll make the rent this month. . . . An' why ain't you takin' a bath?"

"I'm hungry, dammit."

"Get in the tub an' start to scrub. I'll bring in the food when it's ready."

"Can you eat in the tub?"

"On a night like this you can. I am. Might even do my homework in there."

Sniffles giggled again. "Aight."

Corey woke up around midnight to find Sniffles hugging him skin to skin as if he was some sort of blankie. It was obvious from the smaller boy's breathing that he was coming down with a cold and might be going to share it. Corey almost pushed him away, but then gently disentangled himself and quietly slipped out of bed. It seemed a little late to worry about catching Sniffles's sniffles. The boy almost always had them, which was naturally how he'd gotten his name. Happily, he smelled better now, after Corey had scrubbed him with hard-water soap and washed his hair with lice shampoo so it fluffed like an Afro explosion. He still resembled a scruffy rat with fingernails like weapons, but at least he was clean for a change.

The streetlamp's glimmer shone in through the window, bathing Corey's little room with a softly sulfurous glow. The apartment was comfortably warm now, and the patter of rain was soothing. Corey found he wasn't sleepy and considered doing the rest of his schoolwork. His dad would be home in an hour or so, and it would be cool to see him . . . something that didn't happen enough since the man was working double shifts. Corey stood for a moment, enjoying the gentle drumming of rain and its watery splash as it poured off the roof. Rain was cool when you were dry and safe inside somewhere.

He glanced at Sniffles resting in peace, then padded to the window. Rainwater trickled down the glass, gleaming like gold in the yellowish light. Droplets clung to a spiderweb, making a necklace of amber sparks. A car rolled past in the flooded street, pushing a wave that swept the sidewalks—a long, ancient car like a black station wagon and almost as big as a truck. A chill ran suddenly down Corey's spine when he saw it was a hearse! The house next door was a funeral home, a rotting Victorian twin to his own, except for a small weathered sign on its porch. But the place had been closed before Corey was born, its windows boarded, its yard a jungle, its paint peeling off in dirty gray scabs. The hearse swung into its buckled driveway, nosing through weeds and years of trash as if death had been taking a long vacation.

Corey eyed the grim vehicle through the wavering curtain of rain and mist. A tall slender figure, dressed all in black, emerged and seemed to scope out the 'hood. It was too dark to see many details, but the shape was clad in a long leather coat and was almost too slim for its height. Corey couldn't see a face, which must have been the color of night beneath a bristle of short dreadlocks. The shadowy movements were masculine, though graceful somehow and suggestive of youth. Casually parting the waist-high weeds, the ebony figure walked to the house, climbed the steps to its high front porch, and vanished into darkness.

"Corey?"

Corey opened his eyes to see his father stripped to the waist and shiny with rain. He glanced at the clock atop the TV, which showed the time as 3:13. His father's old coat and blue work shirt were hung on a hook above the fire, stained with mud, softly dripping, and sending up spirals of earth-scented steam.

"Why ain't you in bed, son?"

Corey found himself sprawled on the shabby old couch in only his skin and without a clue. He dimly remembered the ancient hearse and wondered if he'd dreamed it. Rain still drummed on the roof overhead, and water still rushed off the eaves. Droplets plunked in the pots and pans, while the garbage cans rattled below. He noticed his history book beside him. "Guess I musta fell asleep. We got a big test on Friday."

"All the more reason you need your rest. Nobody got time to be stupid 'round here." The man frowned a little, hearing a cough from Corey's room. "I been in to see him. Boy got a fever. . . .

Son, we gotta do somethin' 'bout him. He been homeless since his aunt passed on, an' he won't axe nobody for help."

"He always axin' me," said Corey.

"That ain't what I meant."

"He's scared of the cops 'cause they beat him up. Can't he stay here for a while?"

The man sat down beside Corey. "You can't get him shots an' buy him a license. Besides, it ain't fair to him. He should be in school an' learnin' things. We best call Social Services."

"He don't eat much," said Corey, before realizing how stupid that sounded. "But they'll lock him up," he added, hoping that made more sense. "At least for a while, an' he's scared of that."

"I'm a lot more scared of what's gonna happen if he keeps livin' out there on them streets."

"But . . . can't he stay here for a while, Dad? Specially since he gots a cold . . . Um, maybe we could adopt him?"

The big man sighed. "There's a whole lot more to raisin' a boy than just how much he eat, son. An' I'm just too tired to explain it now."

"I guess it's hard diggin' holes in the rain."

"Just keep them grades up an' you'll never find out." The man sighed again and rubbed his eyes, reddened from too little sleep. "All right, Corey. Till he get better." He pulled out a sad-looking wallet. "Go to the store in the mornin'. Get some chicken-noodle soup an' a quart of orange juice. An' fix him some honey-lemon tea like I done for you last year."

"Thanks, Dad." Corey hugged his father, all stony muscle and cold from the rain, smelling of wet dirt and sweat.

"Lord," said the man, rising and stretching. "No rest for the wicked on this earth, boy."

Corey laughed. "You ain't wicked."

"Musta done somethin' wicked sometime, but damn if I know what it was. Y'all get a blanket an' sleep out here. Nobody got time for bein' sick. . . . How's them grades?"

"I let you know on Friday. 'Night, Dad."

"'Night, son." The man started for his room.

"Dad?"

"Yeah?"

"Did you see a hearse out there, comin' home?"

"Matter of fact. Maybe that death house back in business." The man studied his hands for a moment, as if noting their muddy fingernails. "Never no shortage of customers."

"Coal Street."

"Huh?" Corey opened his eyes and blinked, surprised to see the sun shining in through the bus's grimy windshield, although it was low in the west. It had also been beaming brightly that morning when Corey had woken up on the couch to hear Sniffles cough in his room. His dad had already left for work, and Corey had gone to the corner market to get the soup and orange juice. The air had smelled clean and fresh for a change; the flooded streets were beginning to dry, and even the ramshackle houses looked better, their faded paint cleansed of city soot.

"You all right, son?" asked the driver, minus his gloves and parka today, and turning to look back at Corey.

"Yeah. Just a little tired is all. No rest for the wicked, I guess."

The man laughed. "Not on this side of the grave anyway."

"Or on this side of them railroad tracks."

The driver glanced at Corey's pack, which was stuffed to bursting with books. "Got me a feelin' you'll be crossin' over. Dyin' is easy, livin' is hard. But where there's life, there's always hope."

"'Long as you stay away from dope." Corey shouldered his pack and descended the steps. "See you tomorrow, Louis."

The evening air was pleasantly warm with maybe a flavor of oncoming spring. Corey peeled off his tight T-shirt, like shedding a worn-out skin . . . he really needed some new ones. The same went for his faded saggers, which couldn't be buttoned all the way. The last rosy rays of the setting sun felt good on his ebony body. He let his jeans slip to dangerous lows and started walking casually home, noting new grass in the sidewalk cracks and a hopeful green in neglected yards, even if they were only weeds. But then he remembered Sniffles and quickened his pace to a trot.

A few minutes later, back on his block, he saw the ancient truck-size hearse parked in the funeral home's driveway. It looked more funny than frightening now, with its bulbous fenders, tons of chrome, and old-fashioned whitewall tires.

Somebody was cutting the weeds in the yard, a slashing shadow as dark as death that swung a savage machete. It was a boy around seventeen. He wore only jeans and big battered sneaks, his long body shining with silvery sweat as if someone had polished a midnight. Despite his slimness, his muscles were hard, though showing less starkly than Corey's. His face was almost more pretty than handsome, with gentle cheekbones, a small snub nose, and full lips at rest in a half-open pout. His hair was a crown of short spiky locks, while his hands and feet looked a little too large, though there was nothing awkward about him. He moved like a stalking cat or a dancer, reaping a harvest of dead yellow thistles with every bright sweep of his glittering blade. He was clearly the long-coated, leather-clad shape who'd arrived in the hearse last night.

If not for Corey's concern about Sniffles, he might have gone over to meet the dude and ask what was up with the old funeral home. The boy seemed too young for an undertaker, but Corey didn't have time for questions.

Sniffles lay wrapped in a blanket, curled up on the couch and watching cartoons as Corey unlocked the apartment door.

"Yo, Sniff, how you feelin'?" asked Corey, dropping his pack on the floor.

The smaller boy coughed. "Aight, I guess."

Corey felt Sniffles's forehead. "You still got a fever. I make you some soup."

"No pizza, huh?"

"I once saw a pizza, it said, 'Pleased to meet ya, but you gotta buy me before you can try me.'"

Sniffles managed the ghost of a giggle.

"You drink lots of orange juice today?" Corey asked.

"Yeah. The whole thing."

"Cool. You be better in no time, man."

"Then what?"

"Huh?" asked Corey, pausing on his way to the kitchen.

Sniffles coughed and pointed to the window, darkening now as night settled in. "Then I gotta go back out there, huh?"

Corey returned to the couch, hesitated a moment, then took Sniffles's hand. "I'll think of somethin'. Don't I always? Just get better. Okay?"

"Sometimes I wish I was dead."

Corey grabbed the younger boy's shoulders. "Don't you NEVER say nothin' like that, fool!"

Tears squeezed out of Sniffles's eyes. "Well, I do."

Corey almost shook the boy, but then ruffled his bushy hair instead. He came pretty close to hugging the kid, but his own body seemed too unforgiving, like it should have been softer somehow. "Look, little man, where there's life, there's hope."

"Who told you that?"

"A magic bus driver." Corey knelt down and met Sniffles's eyes. "I'll think of somethin'. I promise. Aight?"

". . . Aight."

"Now blow your nose an' wipe your face. Nobody got time for cryin' 'round here."

Corey finished his homework around ten o'clock, clad only in jeans at the kitchen table, then went to his room for a peep at Sniffles. The boy was asleep, but his breathing was stuffy. His forehead felt hotter, too. "Damn!" muttered Corey. "You ain't gettin' outta here that easy, man!" He tucked the blankets a little tighter, then remembered something his father had done when he'd had a cold the year before. He checked his pockets for lunch money: seven dollars and forty-eight cents, supposed to last until Friday. Then he slipped on his sneaks and went out.

He found a jar of Vicks VapoRub at the little corner market . . . he'd massage the stuff onto Sniffles's chest, and that would make him better.

The funeral-home boy must have worked all evening, Corey thought as he hurried past; the weeds were gone from the little front yard and the boards removed from the house's windows. The power must have been restored, and dim light shone through a wine-red curtain. Corey noticed a slim dark shape at rest on the shadowy porch. The boy was still shirtless in nothing but jeans and seemed to be sipping a forty-ounce. Corey wished he could join him.

"Corey?"

Corey woke up on the couch. It was close to 3:00 A.M. The air was scented with VapoRub, but it hadn't helped Sniffles's cough.

"Son," said Corey's father. "If he ain't better tomorrow, we got to call Social Services."

Corey listened to Sniffles's breathing. There was something very lonely about a child's cough in the night. "Yeah, Dad. I know. . . . But maybe he be okay by then. Like, where there's life, there's hope."

"There ain't no hope in a grave, son. I'ma be home at six tomorrow, 'fore I start the other shift."

Corey sighed. "Aight."

"Coal Street . . . Feelin' better 'bout life today?" asked Louis, swinging the bus to the curb.

Corey glanced out at the evening sunlight: The shabby neighborhood yards were greener, lawns were making a pretense of life, and little wildflowers were budding in trash. But his stomach grumbled from lack of lunch, and he scowled while snagging his pack. "Just keep gettin' worse."

"Look for the light at the end of the tunnel."

Corey shrugged. "With my luck, it just be a train. See you tomorrow, Louis."

He didn't stop to take off his shirt but ran home as fast as he could. He arrived out of breath, his chest muscles heaving, which finally burst the worn-out cotton as if he'd been slashed with a knife. "Damn!" he muttered, yanking out his skeleton key and jamming it into the lock. In spite of his rush, he paused in the doorway, seeing the ancient hearse roll up and silently stop in the funeral home's drive. The boy must have spent the day planting roses, which seemed to be blooming all over the yard. Corey recalled the savage figure swinging his long deadly blade: It was funny to think of him planting flowers.

He watched the tall slim shape emerge like a shadow defying the daylight. The boy was wearing his long leather coat, but shed it now to reveal he was shirtless. Then he opened the hearse's big back door. Corey saw it was full of more flowers . . . and something else.

A coffin!

Corey suddenly shivered, even though he was shiny with sweat. The coffin was "classically" shaped, he supposed . . . his father called them "toe-pinchers." It was made of beautiful ebony wood with gleaming brass handles and polished fittings, though it looked disturbingly small.

For all his willowy slenderness, the funeral-home boy seemed surprisingly strong, hefting the coffin onto his shoulder and bearing it into the house. He almost lost his jeans on the way, but that didn't seem funny because of his burden. Corey shivered again as the boy disappeared. He remembered something he'd read in a book, about somebody walking over your grave.

He studied the funeral home once more: Its yard looked pretty with all the new flowers, and the boy had started to paint the front. It would soon be the best-looking house in the 'hood, though its customers probably wouldn't care . . . at least not the ones who would ride in the hearse. Corey thought of the ebony coffin: Did the boy have some business already? Or was it just a sample? Maybe that's why it was small?

He expected Sniffles to be on the couch, but the kid wasn't there, and the TV was dead. Running into his room, Corey found the bed empty . . . and Sniffles's raggedy clothes were gone.

"Damn you!" yelled Corey, clenching his fists, punching the pillow, and kicking the bed for no logical reason. Then he heard footsteps climbing the stairs. "Sniffles?"

But his father appeared in the doorway. "What's up, son?"

"He's gone!" bawled Corey. "Damn little fool! Maybe he heard us talkin' last night?"

The man looked troubled. "He ain't in no shape to be out on them streets. . . . What happened to your shirt?"

Corey glanced down at his chest. "It was old an' wore out . . . like everything else!" He ripped off his shirt and flung it away. "I know where Sniffles cribbed sometimes." He started for the staircase, almost pushing past his father.

The big man sighed and glanced at his watch, a cheap and childish plastic thing. "Call me at work if you find him."

"Coal Street . . . So, how y'all feelin' 'bout life these days?"

It was raining again and dark as night. The bus's windows were all steamed up, and Corey had been gazing at nothing. He shrugged as he picked up his backpack, a book poking out through a rip in a seam as if it was seeking escape. "Life sucks."

Louis paused before opening the doors. "What's the alternative, son?"

"I ain't even sure. . . . You believe in heaven or somethin' like that? With harps an' wings, an' streets made of gold?"

Louis smiled beneath his dark hood, flipping the door switch several times before it finally worked. "Maybe they got better buses up there. But you gotta believe in somethin', son. If you don't, then there ain't no alternative." He reached out to touch Corey's arm. "Still ain't found your little homey? I been keepin' my eye out every day."

"No, an' it been a whole week." Corey looked out at the pattering rain. "An' he was real sick when he left."

"I been watchin' the paper," said Louis. "In case . . . you know?"

"Yeah. I been checkin' the news on TV. But they might not even say nothin'. Not for a little rag-ass like him."

"Tomorrow's always a brand-new day."

Corey tried to smile. "An' April showers bring flowers in May. See you tomorrow, Louis."

Corey was already soaking wet, so there wasn't any reason to hurry. He trudged along, splashing through puddles, and finally arrived on his block. Mist was creeping in from the bay, and the dim streetlamps wore halos again as he passed the ancient funeral home. He hadn't been paying much attention—not this week, out looking for Sniffles before and after school every day— but the long-dead lawn had been reborn, and the old house shone with a new coat of paint. Rosebushes lined the cracked sidewalk and bloomed in beds along the porch, while a white picket fence had been erected, and climbing vines were checking it out. In a way it seemed almost funny, but a few other people along the street had also been raising up new lawns and even planting flowers.

Corey hadn't had the time to meet his dark new neighbor. The dude seemed to rise with the sun every morning, clad in nothing but jeans and sneaks while resurrecting the ramshackle house. He'd taken the faded old sign off the door, and except for his ominous ride out front, no one would have guessed that he lived with death.

Rain rattled down on the night-colored hearse, while its chrome glittered bright in a streetlamp's glow. PACKARD was spelled on its grinning grillwork, though Corey had never heard that name and thought it might be Japanese.

Despite the rain, Corey paused for a moment to study the tall, narrow house. It was dark except for one rear window, a feeble light glowing behind somber drapes. Corey pictured the slender boy, a near-naked savage when swinging his blade, a little bit scary when toting a coffin, and yet he seemed gentle somehow. It showed in his delicate face when he smiled, and in his large and long-fingered hands when he smoothed the earth in his new flower beds.

Corey hadn't thought of it, but he should have asked the boy about Sniffles—after all, he'd been working outside and might have noticed the kid. The one lonely light decided his move: Corey walked to the house past the white picket fence and the nodding rows of rain-sparkled roses. Climbing the steps to the shadowy porch, he softly knocked on the door.

To his surprise, it swung open a little. He almost expected a hair-raising creak, but the boy had probably oiled the hinges. A funeral home shouldn't have spooky doors, but the 'hood was no place to leave one unlocked.

"Um, hello?" he called.

There was only the steady drumming of rain and its trickling splash from the roof. Maybe the boy was taking a nap? As hard as Corey had seen him work, he probably slept like the dead.

"Yo!" called Corey, louder this time. "Your door was unlocked!"

Still no reply. Corey stood there, unsure what to do, while his sodden coat dripped on the new doormat, which logically didn't say welcome. Heavy curtains shrouded the windows, and Corey could see almost nothing inside, except for the shape of a pale chandelier that hung from a vaulted ceiling. But there was probably nothing to see—the house had been empty for decades. The air smelled musty, of dry rot, dust, and free-roaming rats. Of course, the boy had been here a week and might have brought in furniture; but the house FELT empty, and Corey's voice echoed.

Now what, thought Corey? He noticed the door had an old-fashioned lock, and his skeleton key might fit. Should he do the dude a favor?

But what if he wasn't home right now and Corey locked him out? Yeah, the hearse was in the driveway, but the boy might be clubbing with friends . . . you wouldn't go cruising around in a hearse.

"Well, damn," muttered Corey. He remembered something Louis had said: "No good deed ever goes unpunished." He hoped it was a joke.

He peered around in the silent darkness and saw a faint glow across the room. It looked like a light at the end of a hall, maybe the one he'd seen from outside.

"Hello?" he called again.

Corey waited another minute, then made his decision and moved toward the light, his steps slow and careful, a hand stretched out. This was a damn good way to get shot! He stopped, glancing back at the half-open door, and wondered if he should leave while he could.

But then he continued across the room, which seemed to be totally empty. A curtain in shreds concealed a doorway, and the glow leaked out through its rips and holes. Corey parted the rotting cloth: Beyond was a hall with doors on each side that ran all the way to the back of the house. It seemed like a strange arrangement, until he remembered where he was. Those were probably viewing rooms. All the doors were closed except one, down at the end of the hall. The dim light shone from there.

Corey wondered again if he should leave before the dark boy capped his ass, but he tugged his pack a little tighter and moved toward the light anyhow. "Yo, man?" he called softly. "I live next door." . . . As if that gave him privileges.

He waited a minute, but nobody answered. Reaching the doorway, he peered inside. There was the coffin! He almost bolted in shock. . . . But maybe it wasn't occupied? The lid was off, though Corey could see only ruby-red silk, which looked disturbingly comfortable. The coffin sat on a rough wooden stand, which probably would have been buried in flowers had there been a body to view. Crimson candles in tall silver holders were burning beside the ebony box.

Then Corey saw the slender boy asleep in an old velvet chair. He was clad in only his earth-blackened jeans, and his long-fingered hands lay curled on his stomach like peaceful ebony spiders. His legs were stretched out, and his big bare feet were resting atop a cobwebby box that bore the word FORMALDEHYDE. On another such box beside the chair were Church's Chicken remains. Corey noted the long leather coat was draped on a hook in a corner.

Corey stood for a moment surveying the room. He recalled a picture he'd seen in a book of someone "sitting up" with a corpse, maybe in case it came back to life. But the only body in here was the boy's—at least what Corey could see from the doorway—his slim chest rising with slow even breaths. The candle glow softly defined his muscles and darkly highlighted his fine-boned face. He was beautiful yet masculine, and that made Corey afraid. He told himself to get out of here . . . the boy had a right to rest, didn't he?

And yet he felt a need to see . . . maybe he'd rest a lot better himself if he knew for sure that coffin was empty? Glancing again at the sleeping boy, Corey crept up to the coffin, wincing at every squish of his shoes.

Another shock ripped through his body, freezing him there for a second. Maybe somehow he'd expected this?

Sniffles was lying inside. Dimly seen in the candlelight, he looked so cared for and clean. Not at all how he'd looked when alive. His hair had been tamed, and sparkled with oil. His fingernails were neatly trimmed, his hands crossed over his childish chest. He was dressed in new clothes: bad-looking saggers, ass-kickin' sneaks, and a black T-shirt that reached his knees. And now he had his very own crib, soft, satin-lined, and just the right size to peacefully rest in forever.

Tears brimmed up in Corey's eyes, blurring his sight in the candle glow. Turning away from the coffin, he studied the boy in the chair again. You'd have to be gentle to deal with the dead. After all, they were helpless.

He had no right to be here, he thought. He couldn't help Sniffles anymore, and maybe he'd even betrayed the kid by fronting hope in a hopeless place. He quietly started to leave, but his book fell out though the rip in his pack and hit the floor with a thud. He froze again, not quite in fear, as the slender boy opened his eyes.

". . . Um," said Corey. "I live next door. I wasn't stealin' nothin'."

The boy only smiled. "I seen you, man. An' Sniffles said you were cool."

"No, I ain't." Corey looked back at the coffin. "I couldn't do nothin' to help him."

"You done all you could."

"It wasn't enough."

"It was more than most people would do."

"Like, there's such a thing as 'a little bit dead'?"

"Ain't seen that yet," said the boy. "An' I been around death all my life, man. But a lotta folks only a little alive, an' they ain't helpin' nobody."

"Neither did I." Corey turned for the door. "Sorry to wake you up."

The slender boy stretched like a casual cat, then dropped his bare feet from the box and rose. "Just takin' a nap before supper. Y'all wanna stay for a spell? You can sit in this chair if you want. Furniture won't be here till next week. That's when my mom an' pops be comin'. We from Mississippi."

"Oh," said Corey, wiping his face and hoping the raindrops were hiding his tears. "That's why you work so hard."

"Wanna go out for some pizza? If y'all don't mind the ride?"

"Thanks, but I ain't very hungry." Corey returned to the coffin. "Pizza was always his favorite food. So, I guess you . . . um, fixed him up yourself?"

"It was a pretty bad cold, but he's all over it now."

"Yeah," said Corey, fighting more tears. "You done a good job. That's how he always shoulda looked."

The boy came over, glanced in the coffin, then studied Corey and suddenly grinned. "Maybe I keep him around for a while an' you can come over an' see him."

"That ain't funny!" Corey snapped back.

But the boy only laughed. "Careful, dawg, you'll wake the dead." Then he reached into the long black box.

Corey stared in something like horror. "The hell you doin' . . . ?"

"Sometimes you can tickle 'em back to life. Then take 'em out for pizza."

A giggle broke out of the coffin.

by •
*Norma
Howe*

BAZOOKA JOE
AND THE CHAOS KID

Frank Marvelli happened to arrive at his sixth-period sophomore Photography-as-Art class before Jenna MacKenzie that afternoon, which gave him a few minutes to formulate a plan. So by the time she appeared at the classroom door, he was fully engaged in the pretext of extracting a thorn (or some other bothersome intrusion) embedded into the palm of his hand. He was still occupied by his fanciful task as Jenna slipped into her assigned seat next to his at the end of the second row.

"Ah!" he exclaimed suddenly, blowing on the surface of his open-faced palm and giving it a few brushing swipes with his fingertips. "Got it!"

Exhibiting not the slightest interest whatsoever in what Frank could have *got*, Jenna slid her bookbag under her chair and removed a pack of individually wrapped pieces of Bazooka bubble gum from her jacket pocket. Then she leaned forward in her seat and smiled at her friend Jessica, who was sitting on the other side of Frank.

"Hiya, Jessica," said Jenna, tearing open the outer wrapper of the bubble-gum package and removing a piece. "Here, catch! Happy Friday."

And then, almost as an afterthought and without comment, Jenna nonchalantly dropped a piece of gum into Frank's still-outstretched palm as well.

After his initial surprise at this meager but unexpected turn-about in her attitude, Frank was quickly overtaken by a rush of excitement. So *what* if his thorn-in-the-palm ruse fell flat? Perhaps *this* could be the salutatory breakthrough he had been dreaming about! For even though they were already two weeks into the new semester, he hadn't been able, as yet, to forge any meaningful contact with her, and she seemed to be blithely unaware of the fact that he was even trying.

For Frank, this stalemate was a major disappointment, since he'd been itching for a chance to get to know her from the first moment he had noticed her in the cafeteria, eating a slice of pizza and carelessly dropping little bits of olives and pepperoni down her sleeve. For a curious and lonely guy who desperately needed a girlfriend at this particular stage in his life, unearthing a candidate who at least resembled his dream girl on the outside was a very auspicious beginning—especially since his taste in girls was so far removed from the norm, yet completely understandable for a kid endowed with a nascent artistic sensibility somewhat akin to a Salvador Dalí or Federico Fellini—a kid who had long ago become enamored not only with the *idea* of a world conceived in chaos and disorder, but with its real-life manifestations as well.

It wouldn't be an exaggeration to say that Frank was overjoyed when Jenna showed up in Mr. Shreve's Photography-as-Art class this term, and he was even more pleased to find her trapped on the end of the row, with himself happily ensconced on her left, thanks to Mr. Shreve's preference for alphabetical seating.

But until now, that's as far as it went. Before class began, Jenna had an exasperating habit of leaning way forward in her chair and visiting with Jessica, an activity that made Frank feel all but invisible, sitting between the two chattering girls like a piece of wilted lettuce in a baloney sandwich. And on the handful of occasions when he had come *this close* to breaking into their conversation, he had made the mistake of hesitating just a trifle too long, thereby missing each and every opportunity.

At least, as Frank soon came to realize, he wasn't faced with the specter of competition from the other guys in class—or from other guys in the entire school, for that matter—a mysterious truth that he found difficult to understand, but not (from his point of view) at all unwelcome.

And as for Jenna herself, from what Frank had observed so far, she seemed not only to be at ease with her own low profile, but was also completely averse to playing the flirty games he observed in most of the other girls at school. In fact, just the day before, as her friend Jessica was giggling and squealing and trading friendly pokes and jabs with the guy sitting in the row ahead of her, Frank caught a sideways glimpse of Jenna, looking on with a bemused expression that seemed to mirror his own admittedly judgmental and slightly jaundiced assessment of this all-too-familiar drill.

Again, then—with careless and indiscriminate flirting ruled out, might this Bazooka Joe Moment be the perfect opening he has been waiting for? (Or was she merely being polite? After all, it would have bordered on rude, wouldn't it, for her to have tossed a piece of bubble gum over to Jessica without offering one to him as well?)

Still, as the milliseconds flew by, the question raced through Frank's mind—was that *all* it was, just a polite gesture from this one-in-a-million girl seated next to him, and nothing more? At any rate, he threw caution to the wind and quickly decided that he'd better seize this opportunity to interact with her while he had the chance. He moistened his lips and blurted a somewhat belated "Hey, *thanks,* Jenna!" with a wide-eyed expression of gratitude way out of proportion to the gift. She answered only with a slightly raised eyebrow and noncommittal nod, while Frank responded to *that* with an embarrassed smile and a one-shouldered shrug. He carefully thumbnailed open this very special Bazooka Joe wrapper, popped the gum into his mouth, and read his Bazooka Joe fortune number twelve of seventy-five: *Treasure what you have, even if it's all junk.*

Wow! Isn't it astonishing how often those so-called fortunes seem to hit the mark—whether they're published without disclaimers in the daily newspaper or printed beneath the cartoons on Bazooka Joe bubble-gum wrappers? Frank would have enjoyed sharing that observation with Jenna, but Mr. Shreve was tapping on his desk now, asking for attention. Frank folded the colorful little gum wrapper with care and slipped it into the watch pocket of his jeans.

"Okay, class. Settle down, please," said Mr. Shreve. "We've got several presentations to view this afternoon, so we'd better get started. First on the agenda is Jenna's study, which she calls *Watery Reflections,* and afterward, as usual, we'll have some quick critiques from you guys out there in the audience. But let me warn you in advance, you're not going to find much to criticize here!"

Frank could hear a little sigh of relief coming from Jenna's direction, and he gave her an encouraging nod, hoping that he wasn't coming on too strong.

"Yes, indeed," Mr. Shreve was saying, "these shots are quite amazing, when you consider they were taken by a fifteen-year-old novice, using a cheap throwaway camera, no less." He glanced over at Kenny Wong, his student assistant this term. "And thanks, Ken, for scanning Jenna's prints and putting them on a disk for us." Then Mr. Shreve turned to address the entire class once again. "Which reminds me, kids—for those of you who did *not* submit your projects in disk form, I must insist that you do so in the future. We can't expect Ken to take on this extra chore for the entire semester. I know that most of you are not using digitals, but scanners are not that difficult to come by, and as photographers, you must keep pace with the technical advances as fast as they occur."

Mr. Shreve nodded in Jenna's direction. "As I was saying, Jenna, I was totally bowled over last night when I previewed your work. Just a fantastic job for your first assignment."

This additional praise elicited a sudden flush on Jenna's pale cheeks and a downward cast of her eyes, as well as a hasty and quite nervy congratulatory pat on her thin shoulder from Frank.

"This is really weird," Jenna whispered to him in response, one hand cupped around her mouth. "I originally signed up for Painting in Watercolors this period, but the class was full. Jeez, I don't even want to *be* here! I mean, how creative can you get with a *camera,* for God's sake?"

Before the recent Bazooka Joe incident, followed by his sudden seizing of the initiative with his risky congratulatory shoulder pat, Frank wouldn't have had the nerve to look directly at her in such close proximity. But now that she was addressing him personally, he felt a certain entitlement to feast openly and legitimately upon her unusual and striking countenance, and in the few fleeting moments before she turned away, he had just enough time to do the straight-on and close-up survey for which he had been aching. By applying himself diligently, he was able to build on his previous evaluation, first noting the pale blue beauty of her slightly watery eyes, framed by wispy lashes barely visible beneath her sparse but unplucked brows. How beautifully unsymmetrical was her face, bordering on lopsided, really, and with a nose just a tad too large for such a tiny chin, which was, for all that, a splendid repository for the sprinkling of tiny eruptions that perfectly complemented those on her forehead. And, oh! How he loved anticipating the sporadic appearance of her ears, as they revealed themselves from among the thin strands of her light yellowish hair whenever the movement and position of her head warranted such an outing. And, yes! The final test she passed with points to spare, for there was not even a smidgen of makeup on that unique face to mar the beauty of its glorious imperfections!

Frank M. Marvelli was on the verge of swooning, and probably would have but for Mr. Shreve's irritating voice breaking into his reverie. "Once again, I'd like to thank Jeff Collins, manager of the Apple Connection on East Main, for donating this state-of-the-art Macintosh computer to Chapman High," Mr. Shreve intoned as Kenny was inserting Jenna's disk into the computer. "All right, then, Jenna," he added, sitting down and giving her the high sign. "It's all yours."

"Well," Jenna began as her ten photos started to appear one by one on the large TV screen at the front of the classroom, "I took these shots mostly around the lake at Morgan Park. The water is always pretty still there, so I was able to get those reflections of the trees all nice and clear, like a mirror, you know?"

Frank's first impression upon viewing the images projected on the screen was simple disbelief. There must be some mistake.

There *had* to be! Those shots, so utterly boring and predictable, devoid of even the slightest hint of creativity, must surely be the advertising samples from Kodak—nothing at all like what he would have expected from a girl like Jenna. But, no—they were her photos all right, as her running dialogue confirmed.

Frank, feeling slightly nauseated, like the time he had eaten three boxes of sugary Cracker Jacks at one sitting, took a deep breath, slid down in his seat, and closed his eyes. God, what a downer. He couldn't believe that her photos could be such perfect examples of schmaltzy Hallmark art at its worst, the sort of mindless pap that, obviously, appealed directly to Mr. Shreve's conventional bourgeois taste.

"And then I went at different times of the day," Jenna continued. "That's how I got those shots of the sunset reflecting in the water and all."

There were no questions for Jenna after her presentation—only a few obvious compliments coming from the more astute students in the class, eager to get on the good side of their teacher.

"Will you please pass this over to Jenna," Mr. Shreve said, handing his written critique to one of the kids in the first row. "And now," he announced, with a bit of a dramatic flare, "for something completely different! Do you have Frank's disk ready there, Ken?" he asked, checking his notes. "I believe this one is called *The Strange and Haunting Beauty of Disorder.* Did I get that right, Frank?"

Frank sensed something in Mr. Shreve's tone that immediately set him on edge. He took a deep breath and sat up straighter in his seat. "That's it," he answered, with just a slight catch in his throat.

The first image appeared on the screen, but it immediately became apparent that something was seriously amiss. Instead of

The Strange and Haunting Beauty of Disorder, what showed up on the screen was a bikini shot of Linda Yee, Kenny's latest girlfriend.

"Oh, jeez!" breathed Kenny as the class broke out in hoots and howls. "Sorry, Mr. Shreve. I seem to have inserted the wrong disk."

"Obviously," said Mr. Shreve drily, more amused than annoyed.

Kenny began riffling through a bunch of disks in his lap, squinting at each one in turn, trying to make out the titles in the dim light.

"Take your time, Ken," Mr. Shreve said, folding his arms and looking up at the ceiling. "We have all day, you know."

Frank, in yet another uncharacteristically bold move, turned to look directly at Jenna again during this slight reprieve. He knew he should say *something* about her presentation, but still, he couldn't bring himself to lie about it.

But Jenna had finished reading her critique by then and beat him to the punch. "See what I mean?" she whispered. "About no creativity in photography? All I did was imitate those photos that Mr. Shreve has posted on the back wall there, and zip—an A."

"You *imitated his photos?*" Frank exclaimed in a stage whisper, all the while filled with a strange mixture of admiration and relief. "Well, gee! That sounds pretty creative to me!" Then, quickly changing his tone to what he hoped was feigned indignation, he added, "But I'm shocked! Really, *really* shocked!"

"Oh, I *am* sorry," Jenna said, flashing him a huge smile, an obviously insincere mea culpa that very nearly sent Frank completely over the edge, for that was the moment when first he noticed that her bottom teeth were slightly out of whack.

Frank was still watching her as she faced the front of the room again, rolling her critique into a tight tube and then nervously twisting it around and around. A moment later, she suddenly leaned forward and turned toward Jessica. But Jenna had to wait a minute to get her attention, since Jessica was busy laughing and talking with the guy in the seat in front of her again.

"Hey, Jessica," interrupted Jenna as Frank looked idly about the room, pretending he wasn't listening. "Can you show me how to scan my pictures and put them on one of those disks for our next assignment? My brother's got a scanner, but I'd have to wait forever before I could get him to teach me how to use it."

"Oh, sorry," Jessica said, with an embarrassed little smile. "I don't know how to do it, either. My dad offered to teach me, but why should I bother to learn when I can get him to do it for me?"

"Oh," said Jenna, leaning back in her seat. "Well, thanks, anyway."

Somewhere deep within Frank's brain, a window of opportunity had suddenly appeared, but try as he might, he just couldn't bring himself to open it. What if he *did* speak up and offer to show her how to scan her pictures, and she declined the offer? That would only cancel out all the real progress he had made so far today! But then, as he was sitting there agonizing, Jenna herself spoke up.

"Hey, Frank," she said, hesitating slightly and pinching her bottom lip between her thumb and index finger. "I was just wondering—"

Frank, so eager to hear her ask what he just *knew* she wanted to ask, couldn't stop himself from urging her on. "Yeah? *What?*"

"Well, I was just going to ask—"

Frank clenched his fists. *Yes? Yes? Go on!*

Jenna's eyes were darting around his face so rapidly now—first on his chin, then his upper lip, and then back again to his chin—that he actually started to become alarmed. What *was* she about to say, anyway?

"Well, what I mean is—" She paused for a second, just long enough to swallow. "Uh, you know," she blurted out, "you *really* could use a shave."

Frank raised one hand to his mouth and muffled a little yelp of surprise. What *happened?* She must have chickened out! Just as he did! Oh, how his heart went out to her! Disappointed, but feeling himself still in the game, Frank took the ball and ran with it.

"I don't know why you'd say that." He gently rubbed his chin with his fingertips. "I just shaved last year, if I remember correctly." He paused a moment, then added quickly, before she had a chance to react, "Well, okay. So I lied. I've never shaved in my entire life, if you want to know the truth. But can I help it if the Marvelli men are late-blooming shavers? Actually," he heard himself say, "my dad never got around to shaving until after I was born!"

Jenna rolled her eyes. "Yeah. Right."

Frank was surprised that he had actually brought his father into this conversation, and he felt a sudden chill, hoping that she wouldn't pursue the subject, for even though his father had died unexpectedly just before Frank's fifth birthday, the wound—so hurtful and deep—was still tender to the touch.

"Frank? Yo, Frank!" Mr. Shreve was calling out. "We're all set here now, and there's your first shot up on the screen. Will you please try to explain to the class exactly what you had in mind when you took these photos?"

Frank inhaled deeply and blinked several times, struggling to come back to the present. "Uh, okay," he said, squinting slightly and focusing his attention on the screen. "These first shots were taken over at the garbage dump on Dempsey Road."

He looked away from the screen then and spoke directly to the kids. "If you've never been there, you really should go, because what they do is, they actually rescue all the stuff that people throw away—at least the stuff that's halfway salvageable—and then they sell it really cheap, right there at the site."

Frank looked back at the screen. "For instance, that huge pile of broken bicycles you see there—all jammed together? Well, that is actually over twenty feet tall! And by standing where I did, I was able to get those two huge mountains of discarded dinette sets and baby strollers there in the background—sort of reminiscent of the pyramids at Giza, in a weird sort of way."

That's when the first giggle erupted, followed by several bursts of outright laughter, prompted, no doubt, by Mr. Shreve's benign expression of false neutrality.

But Frank, undaunted, held his ground. He remained quiet as the rest of his garbage-dump pictures appeared on the screen, since they were, he believed, self-explanatory. He was still convinced that the photos he had taken there were not only extremely artistic, in an edgy, avant-garde kind of way, but, perhaps more importantly, that they also demonstrated his own personal outlook on life—which was that chaos and disorder are the norm, and should be embraced rather than fought.

"Now, have any of you ever taken a really close look at a sidewalk?" he asked as his final entries appeared on the screen. "Because if you haven't noticed it by now, let me point out that most public sidewalks are *not* clean and neat and newly swept. As you can see in this close-up of the sidewalk in front of school—the sidewalk you walk on every day—well, they're more often full of cracks and weeds and big black blobs of discarded chewing gum and smashed cigarette butts, plus the usual bits of dust and paper and the occasional—I shudder to say it—the occasional disposable diaper. Now *that* is the *true* nature of sidewalks, and *that's* what I wanted to, uh"—Frank hesitated, searching for the right word— "uh, to *capture* in this photograph."

The room was relatively quiet now—with a few of the kids sitting in more or less stunned silence, scratching their ears and rubbing their chins, while the others were half grinning and waiting for their teacher to come in for the kill.

"Well! Any questions or comments?" asked Mr. Shreve, quickly scribbling a few words on his critique form. Frank steeled himself in preparation for the attack. But to his surprise, the room remained quiet.

Mr. Shreve shrugged. "Okay, then, let's just proceed with our next presentation."

But there was a girl in the second row raising her hand, and then lowering it, and then raising it again. "Yes, Jenna!" said Mr. Shreve. "You have a comment?"

Jenna cleared her throat as Frank turned and stared at her. "Well, personally, I thought his presentation was really good," she said. "It was different, you know? Especially those shots of the sidewalk. I mean, I've never looked at a sidewalk from that low, low angle before, and taking pictures of it is something that never would've occurred to me." Jenna turned her head to meet Frank's surprised gaze. "In a way," she added, speaking directly to him now, "your photos are even more—uh, creative than paintings, because they're real, but they don't look real, if you know what I mean."

Jenna glanced back at Mr. Shreve then and raised both shoulders in a self-deprecatory shrug, adding in a calculatedly meek and conciliatory tone, "But then, what do I know?"

Mr. Shreve pursed his lips and nodded thoughtfully. "Okay,

Jenna. Thank you for that. I think you've given us all a slightly new perspective on Frank's work." He glanced down at the critique in his hand and hesitated slightly, as if he might write something more, but then he folded the paper in half and strode over to Frank and handed it to him with no further comment. "Now, class, about your next assignment—" he began.

Frank began to read the critique and groaned slightly when he saw his grade—a bold and circled C minus. With a disappointed frown and a slow shake of his head, he began to decipher Mr. Shreve's hastily scribbled note: *You've got a pretty good grasp of the technical aspects here, but your subject matter is both depressing and easily forgotten.* At the bottom of the page, Mr. Shreve added: *Is this your idea of a joke, Frank?*

"What'd he give you?" Jenna whispered while Mr. Shreve was answering a question about their next assignment. Frank handed her the critique just as the bell sounded.

Jenna quickly read it over twice and then handed it back to him with a sympathetic sigh. She tilted her head toward where Mr. Shreve was still standing next to his desk. "Really pa*thetic*, isn't he?" she said softly. "But hey, I don't think you got our next assignment, did you?"

He shook his head. "No. What is it?"

She stood up and pulled her shoulders back in a quick stretch. "He said he wants us to *tell a story* in ten portraits, using real people. He wants to see a definite beginning, middle, and end— a real *drama*, he said. Like a defining moment in one person's life."

Frank, still quietly fuming about his C minus, managed a grunt and a nod.

Jenna stooped over and pulled her bookbag out from under her chair. Then she glanced up at Frank and held his gaze for just a moment, stroking her chin. "Actually, I think I might be getting a great idea for my own project," she said, squinting at him in such a new and personal way that he felt immediately empowered to ask her what had been on his mind since the beginning of the period.

"Listen, Jenna, if you want, I can show you how to scan your prints and put them on a disk, since I heard you telling Jessica that your brother might not want to, and everything."

Jenna just stared at him for a moment, as if she wasn't quite sure that she had heard him correctly. "You mean—uh, like at your house, or something?"

Hearing the hint of nervousness in her voice only served to make Frank's resolve all the stronger. "Yeah, that would work. Like maybe on Sunday afternoon? Or tomorrow, even. Whenever you can make it."

"Well, I'll have to see if I can get a ride and stuff—"

"Sure," Frank said, his heart pounding a mile a minute now. This was *so* easy! "I'll check with my mom, too. What's your phone number? I'll give you a call tonight, and we can set it up."

Since his mother wasn't home from work yet, Frank let himself in the front door and immediately stumbled over a stack of old newspapers that he had neglected to take out to the recycling bin, in spite of his mom's constant reminders. Last week's pile of laundry, which he was supposed to have folded and put away, had overflowed the couch and was now strewn across the front-room floor, and a couple of lopsided grocery bags still containing packages of pasta and cans of chili beans were sitting in front of the TV like faithful viewers waiting for their favorite show. Somewhere, under a disheveled pile of magazines and paperback books, CDs and videos, a couple of shriveled apple cores stuffed into an empty Cracker Jack box, and a pair of garden shears, there surely must have been a coffee table, but at the moment it was nowhere to be seen.

Frank made his way to the refrigerator and, after eyeing the precarious situation on the drain board, proceeded to put a wobbly stack of dirty plates in the dishwasher before they toppled into the sink. Tidying up the kitchen was his job, but he felt no sense of urgency, even though he knew that he was about due for another halfhearted motherly reprimand. However, he was more than ready for her this time, with an inspired analogy comparing their perpetually cluttered kitchen to contemporary music: *Chaos is the norm, Mom! It's the natural state of the universe. And it's beautiful. Like modern music—all dissonant and confused. The struggle for orderliness and neatness is a lost cause, so why do you continue to fight it?*

Frank was never quite sure whether his mother's willingness to let things slide was due more to his superpersuasive arguments or to her reluctance to rock the boat, so to speak, since in all other respects, he knew that she regarded him as an ideal son. Although he sometimes found himself wondering if perhaps he wouldn't be able to actually "live his philosophy" so relatively unhampered if his father were still alive, those notions always brought on such a mixture of sadness and guilt that he quickly turned to other thoughts.

Frank put a few more dishes into the dishwasher and then began to rummage around in the refrigerator. He soon found a can of soda behind a plate of leftover chicken and headed toward his room. With the slanted beams of the afternoon sunlight sneaking in through the dusty surfaces of his droopy window blinds, he cautiously nudged the door open a few more inches and started making his way toward his bed—sloshing through a swamp of crumpled papers and bunched-up underwear, miscellaneous rocks from an old collection, dirty socks and sweatshirts, holey old shoes and books and extension cords, misplaced components of discarded speakers, neglected notebooks filled with drawings of trees and spiders and other interests of the past, a catcher's mitt, candy wrappers, broken pencils and Bic pens, scattered playing cards, dead batteries, and little soaps from the Vagabond Motel. Fearlessly, he high-stepped his way through a concentrated area of disabled kites and model airplanes like an intrepid scientist courageously forging a path through the tangled rain forests of Borneo in search of some yet undiscovered species of plant life from which a cure for malaria might be derived. Almost there now, still undaunted, Frank stumbled and pitched his way through the final few feet of his journey, homing in on an indistinguishable mound against the wall that he knew must be his bed. And in the final, fleeting moment before he reached his destination, his dark eyes swept across the room, and he caught his breath as he viewed the unique array of chaotic beauty laid out before him in all its most wild and primal splendor.

With a lovingly gentle sweep of his lean and not-yet-manly arms, Frank leveled out a little nest for himself amid the junk on his bed, ignoring the tinkles and clunks of whatever objects found themselves suddenly cast aside. With dead-on accuracy, he immediately located his pillow buried within the sheets and blankets and then plopped down on the bed with a long and drawn-out sigh of contentment and relief, carefully reaching over and placing the soda can on top of an old wicker birdcage he had rescued from the dump. But, as usual, he couldn't avoid focusing directly on the huge and faded red-and-silver banner hanging on the opposite wall.

WARNING!
THIS IS THE PRIVATE ROOM OF
FRANKIE THE FEARLESS
ENTER ONLY AT YOUR EXTREME PERIL!

Fashioned by his father when Frank was only four, the sign had done its duty throughout all the intervening years, faithfully guarding and protecting little Frankie against all manner of villains and evil spirits lurking in his room, from the scary moose in his picture book to the unspeakable horrors originating in his own imaginative mind. And, as his father had so unwittingly suggested, if the large sign and his proud name were not enough to do the job, the evil ones would most certainly trip and fall to their deaths on the ever-growing pile of toys and junk scattered like booby traps about his floor.

Frank's moment of repose was short-lived, for he suddenly remembered the bubble-gum wrapper from Jenna, still folded up in the pocket of his jeans. He sat up, retrieved it with his fingertips, and reached above his headboard, feeling for a stray thumbtack among the myriad *Life in Hell* cartoons that he has been clipping out of the newspaper for years. Finally locating a tack, he began to pry it out, all the while pressing his other hand flat against the wall, hoping to secure as many cartoon panels and other miscellaneous clippings as possible until he was able to reinsert the thumbtack—this time with the addition of the Bazooka Joe wrapper.

Success! The only loss was a tiny printed slip of paper from inside a fortune cookie—Frank's all-time favorite: *Beautiful is in the eyes of the bee-holder*. Oh, well. Let it go. Frank watched, fascinated, as his fortune fluttered downward in a randomly whirling pattern on its death flight to oblivion.

Lying on his back then, and clasping his hands beneath his head, Frank turned his gaze along the walls of his room and experienced once again that familiar feeling of inner peace and joy. He never tired of the sight—for there was his life: the fading photos and the tattered-edged airplane posters, the yellowed clippings and cutouts overlapping one another like desiccated butterfly wings, as well as the lacy remains of genuine butterfly wings clinging to their rusted pins, the abundant and various non-awards and meaningless citations printed on fake parchment and passed out through the years like candy, the once-treasured baseball and other collector's cards, and his fabulous movie posters, plus the unidentifiable accumulation of flotsam and jetsam extending all the way back to his first drawing of a dinosaur in Ms. Knight's kindergarten class. Oh, what a work in progress of stupefying proportions and unbelievable artistry were the walls of his room!

Frank could hardly wait for his mother to start making dinner that evening, since he planned to tell her about Jenna then, and he wanted to get past that hurdle as soon as possible.

Finally, after changing her clothes, reading the mail, and making a few phone calls, she joined him in the kitchen. "So, what'll it be?" she asked, bending over and peering into the refrigerator. "There's some leftover chicken here. I can either warm it up or make a cold chicken salad—"

"Whatever," Frank said. "But listen, Mom—this girl in my photography class wants to come over this weekend and—"

"Ouch!" exclaimed his mother, raising her head so fast that she bumped it on the refrigerator doorframe. "What did you say?"

"This girl at school—she needs to learn how to scan her prints and burn them on to a disk." Frank shrugged, hoping his mother wouldn't try to make a big deal out of this. "So I said I'd show her how. Sometime this weekend. That's all."

"Oh," his mother answered, ducking her head back into the refrigerator—but not soon enough to hide from Frank the sudden flush on her cheeks.

Okay, Frank thought. *Just play it cool.* He quickly rubbed his nose and cleared his throat. "So how about tomorrow afternoon, then? Like about two o'clock?"

His mother removed the plate with the chicken and placed it on the counter. Then she slowly sat down at the table, opposite Frank. She looked at her watch and rubbed the back of her neck. Then she started fiddling with her wedding band, twirling it around and sliding it up and down her finger, the way she did when she was thinking about things and considering her options.

Frank, for his part, stayed calm and began to reexamine the recent site of that bothersome thorn in his palm. Did he *really* manage to get all of it removed?

Finally, his mother spoke. "Listen, Frank," she said. "I don't believe you'll have time to catch up on your chores by tomorrow afternoon."

Frank looked up, sincerely puzzled. "My chores? What do you mean?"

"What do I mean?" his mother asked, her voice rising slightly. "I mean you can't have a guest over here when the house looks the way it does."

"But you don't say anything when my friends come over," he protested, not bothering to mention that they still remarked on how lucky he was to have a mother who let him get away with murder.

"Well, that's my mistake, for not laying down the law sooner, I guess."

"But why now? What's so different about—"

His mother stood again and began fussing with the chicken. "Frankie," she said, "it's just *time*. You're growing up now, and it's just time, that's all." She opened the refrigerator again and got out a couple of tomatoes. And then she reached for her paring knife and shook it in his general direction. "So you've got some major picking up to do before that girl comes over."

"Okay, okay! I get it!" he joked.

His mother grinned and started to slice a tomato.

Frank spread his arms wide in a gesture that included the entire house, and in a last-ditch attempt to salvage whatever he could from this sudden and alarming turn of events, he implored, "But do I *really* have to disturb this beautiful and wonderful natural state of chaos?"

His mother's stern look said it all.

But it also set Frank to thinking. Could his mother be right about this? Frank looked past her and into the front room. Would Jenna actually think *less* of him, once she was admitted to the inner sanctum of Clutter Castle? He couldn't be sure, but there was no way out of it now. "Oh, boy." He sighed. "It'll take me all day tomorrow, at least."

"At least."

"So what if I call her and tell her to come over on Sunday afternoon then, instead of tomorrow?"

His mother nodded. "Fine. As long as you intend to keep your end of the bargain."

Frank sensed that he might have a slight edge now, so he decided to play it for all it was worth. "Naturally, we're only talking about the *public* spaces here, right? I mean, my own room is still exempt, isn't it?"

His mother rolled her head around with an exasperated expression and let out a big sigh, which Frank, of course, took to mean yes.

After dinner, Frank walked through the house and began to survey the extent of the problem. Since the computer was in a little alcove off the dining room, and because the front room and kitchen were also in view, he'd have to clean them all.

And then there was the problem of the bathroom in the hall. Certainly, his mother saw it in an entirely different light, but to Frank it was nothing less than a masterpiece of benign neglect, and he recoiled at the thought of putting it in order. Jenna would be in the house for only a short time, he told himself, so he would act on the assumption that she wouldn't be venturing into that particularly interesting venue.

Frank wasn't at all nervous when he called Jenna later that evening, and they agreed that she'd arrive at his house around 2:00 P.M. on Sunday.

He rose early the next morning, and once he got into the swing of things, the housecleaning went better than he expected. He had the kitchen all spruced up and the junk in the other rooms picked up and put away by late that evening. All he had left to do was the vacuuming, but he could finish that up in the morning. (Of course, if his mother happened to open the door to the hall closet or check under the skirted couch in the front room, he was dead meat.)

Jenna caught on to the scanner and its application in record speed, which didn't surprise Frank in the least, and he could tell that she appreciated his patient and easygoing tutoring skills. On several occasions their fingers happened to meet on the mouse and somehow managed to remain there together for inordinate periods of time. Frank considered it a hopeful sign that she didn't seem to be at all uncomfortable with that degree of intimacy.

All too quickly they were sitting side by side on his front steps, waiting for her father to come pick her up. "Your mom's real nice," Jenna remarked, leaning over and pulling up her socks.

"Yeah, I guess she's okay." Frank grinned, feeling right at home now. "Except that she made me straighten out the house before you came."

"Really? Sounds like my mom. But I kind of like things neat, too." Jenna paused a moment. "You know, Frank," she continued, "I've been wondering—I mean, I've been thinking about our next assignment—you know, Mr. Shreve's defining-moment, story-in-portraits thing? And I've been toying with this terrific idea I got—"

"Really? What is it?"

"Well, remember when he said we might enlist a classmate to use as our model?"

Frank's heart almost flew out of his chest, it was beating so fast. "No, I didn't hear that."

"Oh. Well, I guess you were still reading your critique and didn't hear him, but that's what he said. Anyway, I want to use you as my model. I want to photograph you at the defining moment of your very first shave."

Frank was suddenly speechless.

"The idea just came to me, like that," she said, snapping her fingers. "After class, on Friday. And once I thought of it, well, I couldn't think of anything else."

"My very first shave?" Frank heard himself say. "You want to photograph me, *shaving?*"

"Yeah! I do. In ten shots."

"Uh—and just where would that take place?" Frank asked, suddenly panicking and fearing the worst.

"Well, here, of course. At your house. Where else? I have it all planned out—with a beginning, a middle and end, like Shreve said." She was speaking very rapidly now, hardly pausing to breathe. "See, it'll start with you just waking up and touching your face, realizing that this is the Big Day. In other words, it's *time!*"

Frank suddenly reared backward, whacking both elbows on the hard edge of the step, but wincing only slightly, hiding the pain. The way she had said *it's time* seemed to echo his mother's words in a strange and uncanny way. But it was the *just waking up* phrase that really put him on notice.

"Did you say *waking up?*" he asked. "Hold it. Waking up in my bed, you mean?"

Jenna sighed and looked annoyed. "No, Frank. Waking up in the bathtub. Of *course* in your bed! Where else?"

"You mean in my *room*—in my bed?"

She looked very confident now, like she could get away with anything. "Sheesh! So what's the big problem? Your mommy will be here, for God's sake. Nothing's going to *happen* to you."

Frank smiled in spite of himself because her words and manner did strike him funny, even though her proposal had the potential for disrupting his entire way of life.

"And then," Jenna went on, all fired up now, "I'll do a few close-ups of you in front of the bathroom mirror, with your face all screwed up like guys do when they shave."

Frank looked a little sick. Oh, damn! Not the bathroom, too!

Jenna grinned. "Don't look at me like that. I have a brother, remember? I know how guys look while they're shaving. I'll take some great angle shots. I can just see them now, in my mind's eye. How about it, Frank? Will you do it?" She paused a moment. "Please?"

Frank's brain was spinning. All that he held dear was suddenly at stake. All his posturing, his love of chaos, and the appeal of disorder in his grand scheme of things—all that, destined to go right out the window. It was almost too much for him to handle.

"So, come on! What's the verdict? Yea or nay?"

"Shreve won't like it, you know," Frank said with a warning squint. "It's much too creative for his taste," he added, pleased with himself for coming up with a plausible argument.

But Jenna only laughed. "Who cares? It would be worth it! And besides, I can easily make it up on other assignments."

Frank shook his head. "Listen, Jenna. This is not as simple as you seem to think. I really need some time to mull this over." He paused a moment, wishing he could be more honest with her. "The thing is, well—there's more here than meets the eye."

Jenna shrugged, then stood up and brushed off her jeans. A couple of squirrels were scampering around the foot of the huge maple tree next to the driveway, and she crouched over a bit and slowly headed toward them, stalking them like a prowling cat.

Frank put his head in his hands and stared at the concrete walk beneath his feet. Sure enough, it was beginning to crack. He looked over at Jenna, who was engrossed in the squirrels. Of course, she had no way of knowing the enormity of what she was asking him to do.

"Here comes my dad," she called suddenly, pointing up the street. "So I'll call you around seven tonight, okay? After you have time to *think,*" she added with a grin, as if his hesitancy were nothing but a comic ploy in this, their prelude to—to what? Only time would tell.

Frank sat on the front step for a long time after she had left, watching the ants traversing the cracks in the sidewalk. After a while, he looked at his watch and decided that he had time enough before darkness fell to blow the leaves off the lawn and out of the flower beds, even though, by doing so, he would be disturbing one of nature's most beautiful examples of chaos in action.

An hour or so later, after he had put the leaf blower back in the garage and washed up, Frank walked a straight path through the neat house and into his own room, closing the door behind him. One glance at the jaunty little Bazooka Joe wrapper hanging perilously by one corner on his wall, and his course was set. He took a final, lingering look and immediately knew where he had to start. With a deep sigh but resolute heart, he reached high up on his wall and removed the red-and-silver banner that his father had made for him so long ago, and at that moment he could almost feel his childhood slipping away like a great ship slowly leaving the pier and heading out to sea.

A little after seven, when the phone finally rang, Frank raised his fists in a sweet and powerful gesture of victory, and rushed to answer it.

● *by*
Marina
Budhos

THE PLAN

Victor knows he's doomed the instant his mother emerges from the subway stop on Flatbush Avenue.

Her long black waves are gone—utterly gone. Instead her hair is a bright yellow, cropped tight against her skull. Gold hoops bounce against her long neck. With her dark, arched eyebrows, she looks good, striking even, like Halle Berry, just who his mom wants to be.

But he's sure, with a dull angry weight in his stomach, what it means. They're moving again.

Victor is still amazed at how his mother can shed one skin, one life for the next, while he drags reluctantly behind. She does it all the time: from Venezuela to Trinidad, from there to the Virgin Islands, and then on to Miami Beach, where he remembers the white glow of her shoes as she left for an early shift cleaning rooms at a hotel. But they chucked that, too, headed north, first to Boston and then lasted four years here in Brooklyn.

But you never know with Esmeralda how long they might

stay in a place. Or Vicki. Or Leela. How many names has she had?

At her latest job, working as an assistant hairdresser in a fancy place in SoHo, they'd given her a white lab coat, for when she handled rinsing out the dye, her Boston name—Vicki—across the right-hand pocket. The first night, she plucked out the red stitching and sewed in *Esmeralda,* telling them it was her middle name. Lately he knew she was getting itchy with that name. "It's too Latin, too foreign—not in a good way," she told him. "It makes them think I'm from the Philippines and all I'll ever be is a hairdresser."

That's what it always was about, of course: who she could be, out there; a new, better version of her, out there. No matter what he thinks.

Irritated, he follows his mother home to their walk-up apartment in a brick row house and he's in for another surprise, tucked in her big black nylon bag: a whole sheaf of new modeling photographs, and printed on them, her new name—Sandi Brown.

Victor doesn't want to hear any more—he has a tight feeling under his ribs. He flops down on the sofa and flicks on the TV. Maybe if he turns the sound up real high, he can drown out her yammering.

"Victor!" She stands in the middle of the room, blocking his view. "Victor, I'm talking to you!"

"Yeah."

"Victor, this is a big one." She presses her palms together. Her nails have been done a coral pink. It disgusts him that he knows stuff like this, but it's hard not to—his mother's hairdressing and beauty magazines are all over the apartment, and sometimes, when he's bored, he reads them.

"Victor, we're moving."

The words drill through him, dully. He's been waiting for her to say it since the subway. Only now news like this doesn't catch in his throat the same way, doesn't give him that small spiral of terror like it did when he was young. Instead it makes him angry because this time, he was starting to feel at home, like he belongs a little. Just today this girl, whom he'd been eyeing for weeks now—Cecilia—talked to him for fifteen minutes. He knows a little bit about her: that she's lived her whole life in a house in Carroll Gardens with her mother and father and kid brother, and their front yard has a metal statue of the Virgin Mary. Every time he sees her in the school yard with her friends, she doesn't break down into stupid giggles. Her eyes are a warm brown, with gold lashes, and she has a way of smiling and listening as he talks. She usually wears a navy sweater tied over her shoulders, a little preppie, unfashionable, but that gives him a good feeling. Today she even walked with him to the bus stop. Now that was progress, he thinks.

"Where to?" he asks his mother.

She brightens. "Don't be silly. You know. California. It's time."

"Uh-huh."

"And there's something else." She drops down on the sofa next to him, wriggles close. She's wearing some kind of striped pants that stop at her calves and a yellow, clingy T-shirt. She looks hot. He knows that because all his friends have kidded him about it. *Man, your mother is so hot, is she a model or something? Sort of,* he would say. *Almost. Wannabe.* For as long as he could remember.

"I've got another idea." And then she leans close and whispers in his ear. He hears every syllable, the words strung together in their audacious chain. Light floods through his head. He feels dizzy, then sick, then dizzy again. But he makes her repeat it.

"That's right." She laughs. "In our next home, you'll be my brother. And I'll be your sister."

It isn't the craziest of ideas. After all, his mom is young. Thirty-four, by last count, but you sure as hell can't tell with that gleaming smooth skin, those tight, sharp features from her Portuguese father. She was nineteen when Victor was born, and most of the time he was growing up, she was growing up along with him.

Victor has never known his father, but he's always heard the story, of when his eighteen-year-old mother worked in a fancy men's boutique in the Inter-Continental Hotel and met a man who bought forty silk ties from her; how he left her with the astonishing sum of twenty thousand dollars, deposited into a bank account with her name. *You will be someone,* he wrote to her, on heavy, cream-colored hotel stationery. She was, by that time, four months pregnant with Victor, and she stared at the gold crest at the top margin and said, "You're damn right I'll be someone."

By now she's been many someones, each a new, light, and golden changeling self—her hair was long, short, bobbed, permed, pinned into an elegant chignon; her dresses full or slinky, short and long. She was a hostess at a fancy restaurant in Curaçao; a tour guide and then a party organizer in Trinidad; even a local reporter on a TV station in the Virgin Islands. Whoever she was, her new name and look would glance across Victor's skin in a reflecting bounce, but not one of them endured, became a part of him. Roommate, buddy, my one and only, *mi querido,* she would whisper to him. She has dozens of nicknames for him, but never this: baby brother.

This is the plan: She's shaving nine years off her life, just like that. They are brother and sister; their parents died years ago in a car crash. She's always supported him, and they've always been together. That will be the story for anyone "in the business."

And at home?

"At home we're ourselves, honey."

And his friends?

She hesitates. "I think it best we don't mix things up, don't you? That we're consistent?"

"But why can't you just be yourself?" he asks. "Why do you have to lie?"

Her chin wobbles; her eyes fill with tears. "You just don't know how hard it is out there," she whispers.

Victor gets up from beside his mother and goes into the bedroom, the only bedroom, actually. His head is spinning. A wet lump lies in his throat, and his eyes sting, as if he's smoked too many cigarettes at a party. It's not as if he ever liked this apartment, any more than the rest. But everything was starting to get easier—he'd even imagined swinging through Cecilia's wrought-iron gate, past the statue, and taking her out on a Friday night.

It isn't that his mother is selfish, he reasons. Wherever they've lived—from the mold-smelling motel room in Miami, where the panes rattled every time a truck blasted past, to the apartment before this one, in a basement where the pipes sighed overhead—she always gave him the best space. He was the one with a bed with a blue corduroy spread. She always made sure to check out the schools and sign him up for anything and everything that was free, and she spent all kinds of money on him—on suede shoes, and music lessons, even a small drum set when he'd gotten it into his head last summer that he wanted to join a band.

About a year ago his mother had gotten serious about her modeling and acting career: She put together a portfolio, went on auditions and shoots when she wasn't at the salon. She'd even landed a few small jobs—nothing terribly glamorous, just some catalog and department-store gigs—enough to show she worked.

But she didn't like how she was typecast—thirtyish mother (even though she looked ten years younger) in subdued striped dresses and dull pumps. "I'm going nowhere but back to Sears and Marshall's with this," she often complained. And so she'd reinvented herself into someone much younger, sexier, and she started going to auditions dolled up in slinky skirts and spandex tops.

That's how she got an agent in California. Some guy named Larry, with an office in Studio City, was visiting New York and spotted her when she went to an open call. They met for coffee after, and he liked what he saw, enough to take her on, though he recommended a name change. She did more than that— she'd gotten herself another set of photos, even sexier, with her new name emblazoned at the bottom: Here she was angled on a stool, in a pair of black satin pants; in another, bent over, her fingers at her neck, in a shimmery, low-cut dress. To think that half an hour over a Starbucks latte meant that Victor's life would be ripped apart, all over again.

He drops down on the bed, holds his arm over his eyes. He is suddenly tired. Bone tired, like an old man. She's never done this.

He's always been her son.

Sandi finds them an apartment like the others: ugly and functional. Since it's California, there's a pool, and since it's summer and Sandi spends most days on auditions or working her new hairdresser job, he swims. Ever since they've gotten here, Victor has been angry, but he works it off doing laps, letting his arms chop the lukewarm water. The pool isn't long—he's across in six strokes—but he can feel his newly tanned arms and legs twined with muscles, growing strong, powerful. Every morning he also does free weights and ab machines in the small gym off the lobby. He imagines getting a girlfriend soon, someone who smells like soap, and listens, like Cecilia; whom he can cradle in his arms, lie with on the sand at Venice Beach, the waves pink in the sunset.

Sandi lavishes on him a new wardrobe: surfer-style shorts that hang low on his hips and red and blue T-shirts, and mesh sneakers that slap the pavement. They buy a car—a green Honda with a dented fender—and weekends they go shopping at Target and Wal-Mart, pick up cheap curtains and stackable, folding furniture, the kinds of things they've bought dozens of times before, and that Sandi is so expert at finding. She circles the ads in the local paper, and they drive around the tonier neighborhoods, pursuing garage and estate sales. They get a double bed— for him again—and an old lady's dresser, lined with yellowed, primrose paper. They eat lunch out, as if practicing their sister– brother act, usually in more upscale places—Venice or Santa Monica. "You related?" a waitress at a sushi restaurant asks them.

"Brother and sister," Sandi says quickly.

"Gorgeous. What a combo," she comments, and at that moment, staring out at the California palms leaning against the ruddy sky, he thinks: It's possible. Everything they say about this place is possible.

When Victor was twelve, it looked as if he'd take after the Portuguese side—short and compact, like his grandfather. He'd get picked on, nothing really bad, but being the new kid didn't make it any easier—an egg splattered against the back of his head, cold yolk sliding down his nape; a girl who pretended to like him, then, when he tried to kiss her, a bunch of guys would descend on him, pummeling his back. Around his fourteenth birthday, he grew taller, a little broader in the chest. His hands spread, his shoulders strained his T-shirts. He noticed in gym he could really whack the punching bag. The freckles across his nose faded, and he began to have the brown glossy skin tone of his mother; his teeth were now straight and clean white. There was around him a halo of specialness, the sense of someone about whom people said, *Didn't I just see that guy in a movie or on a poster for toothpaste or something?*

That is their curse, he thinks now, jabbing at his sushi roll. They do look good. Like people, mother and son, brother and sister, on whom fortune—money, Hollywood, whatever they wanted—should shine, gloriously.

By Sunday night they're both exhausted, from all the moving and rearranging and thinking through what their new home should look like. He goes for a swim then, donning a towel over his shoulders, and by the time he returns, his mother is in her terry robe, ironing her outfit for the next day.

One weekend, after their usual rounds of garage sales, his mother turns into a nearby mall, to the liquor store, and comes out with a bottle of red wine in a paper sack. "What's that for?" he asks.

She smiles—a crooked, charming smile, her teeth flashing almost indecently—the look they say will get her on a million commercials. "Larry's coming over."

His heart does a skip. He feels weak around the knees. "Larry?" He fiddles with the air-conditioning vent, turns it up, until the stream of air pushes against his throat, as if it's a kind of gargle, so he can practice: *Hi, Larry. I always wanted to meet my sister's agent.*

"When?"

"Tonight."

"Jeez." The air now prickles.

"Oh, Victor." His mother turns to him, puts her palm on his knee. It's warm and dry. "I'm sorry I didn't tell you before. It's not a big deal. Really. Larry's a friend, too."

"He's your agent. And your friend. I'm your son and your brother. Does everybody double up these days?"

"Mi querido." Sandi tips her head, lets it rest on his shoulder. There should be a girl doing this, Victor thinks, a girl who isn't fickle like my mother but just stays there, stays still, while we watch the waves move.

"Forget it," Victor says, and pulls away.

Larry is old. Not old-old, but not some up-and-coming hotshot, for sure. Victor picks up a sour smell about him: someone who's been haunting the L.A. studios for too long and hasn't completely cracked them. His voice is a tired lisp; he wears a black T-shirt belted into nubby blue pants. His face is chiseled to a point with a graying goatee. "You looking forward to school?" he asks Victor while Sandi's in the tiny kitchenette making pasta and clam sauce and cutting up slices of mozzarella on tomatoes.

"I guess."

"The schools here aren't that bad. My kids did public straight through. Then they creamed me for college tuition, wouldn't go to a California school."

So he *is* old, Victor thinks.

"By then a few of my clients were on regular TV gigs, so I could afford it." He nods his head toward the kitchen. "Like your sister there. She'll be paying my retirement, that's for sure."

Victor thinks it's weird that he's confessing his money woes, and he wonders if Larry thought he was Sandi's son, would he speak differently? She's still busy in the kitchen. He gives Victor a thin smile, wipes his hands on his knees. Then Victor realizes: He's uncomfortable. How many twenty-five-year-old aspiring actresses live with their fifteen-year-old brothers? Sandi may have dyed her hair and come up with a good story, but it's a story that makes people awkward, twitchy, and a little sad. For a second, Victor feels sorry for his mother, is roused out of the groggy anger he's felt ever since they've moved here.

"Voilà!" Sandi sweeps in, the platter held aloft. It's got a chip on the blue rim—another yard-sale find—which she turns ever so slightly, away from Larry's gaze. He doesn't notice, though. His eyes are all on Sandi: on the way she flicks off the apron and then doles out the mozzarella; how she tilts her head when she laughs. He tells her, over and over, it's going to be so easy getting her gigs; she's one of the easy ones.

Poor Larry, Victor thinks. He looks like a chemistry teacher at his high school. Sincere, hardworking; he hooks on to his clients for good—they make him feel glamorous, a little bigger than himself.

"So what made you want to be an agent for my"—Victor chokes it out—"my sister?"

Larry smiles. "That's simple. When I met her in New York, I was seeing around two hundred people. But there's something about her. Very natural. Unaffected. As if she could take it or leave it. What a relief. You have no idea how directors can smell the desperation. The audition rooms reek of it out here."

"That's because I have a life," Sandi says, nodding toward Victor. "I have to make sure he goes to school and is okay and everything else."

Larry flushes, parts his mozzarella and tomato with a knife. "I think it's amazing, how you two have stuck together." He grins at Victor. "Isn't she amazing?"

Victor doesn't answer. He's thinking of that phrase: *stuck together*. Yeah, that's what we are. What he wants to ask is, *Do you always come to dinner with your clients?*

As if reading his mind, Larry goes on. "Even my being here. I thought it was so sweet. Your sister and I were supposed to have a business dinner, strategize about auditions now that she's here. But she was worried about you being all alone."

Even her casualness, Victor thinks, is a big act. After all these years, she's gotten so good at it, she has her own agent fooled.

Larry forks a bit of cheese into his mouth and continues. "In this town, you have no idea how rare that is. That means a lot to me. I have this thing with my clients. A pact. Never lie. Never bullshit me. Tell me if you've cheated on your wife or you're back on cocaine. But don't lie. That's the end of the end."

Sandi and Victor exchange glances. His mother looks tired and strained to him; he can see the half crescents around her eyes, like parentheses. Victor shakes his head, as if to say, *You're asking for trouble.*

"Eat your salad," she says sharply.

Larry doesn't stay too long, though after dinner, when Victor is swimming in the pool, he can hear the soft tinkle of their voices on the balcony.

For a brief moment, as he plies the blue water, he thinks he smells the sweet smoke of pot, but then he realizes it's just eucalyptus mixed with tire rubber, from the outside. Sandi would never smoke. She's straight as can be in that department.

There was a year, when they were living in Cambridge, and Sandi was working as a receptionist, rolling her feet into stockings and pulling on a gray skirt every day, straightening her hair, that he smoked a lot of pot. That move had been hard, breaking into his new school. He figured the only way he could survive was if he picked the toughest band of boys and smoked weed with them on the corner. Suddenly he wasn't the stiff new kid in the neighborhood. Goofy words sprang out of him; he did silly things. He cartwheeled down the pavement. He told stories— about his mother and all her crazy lies and lives—and everyone ate it up.

After, he'd come home and raid the cupboards and fall asleep in front of the TV. When he woke, his head would ache, and he'd feel dirty about telling her secrets. But he couldn't stop. Until one day, he was doing his goofball act, telling them about Leela, the Reporter Girl, who didn't know anything about the news, when he heard a cough behind him. It was his mother, dressed in her sober gray secretary skirt and pumps, her hair pinned back. In her hand was his report card—all lousy grades, since he slept through most of his classes, anyway.

That night, he heard her sobbing in the bedroom. He had broken her heart, and that was the first time he realized his mother really cared, not just about her future, but about his, too. After that, she began plotting her escape from their bad neighborhood and her dreary job—she went to hairdressing school at night and began calling the board of ed in New York, to see about some decent schools down there.

By the time Victor has taken his shower and dried off, Larry has gone and his mother is cleaning up in the kitchen. She's very quiet and still, as if having Larry over has done something, sealed them into their new life. The air feels dangerous between them. After he's toweled off, Victor stands in the kitchen doorway, watching her load the dishwasher.

"Are you okay, honey?" she asks him, without looking up.

"Yeah. Sure. Why not?"

"Larry's a nice guy, isn't he? Not one of those creeps."

"Sure."

"He liked you. Said you were very mature. We both are. That he can't imagine how I took on a nine-year-old boy, just like that. I told him that there's a lot we can do, we just don't realize it."

"Ma, that's a story."

She looks up, and sees a trickle of suds caught on her new, sand-colored locks. "I *know* that, Victor. But it's still true."

School is easier than he expected—there's something about it always being good weather here, sauntering past the rosebushes into the open-air buildings, milling around in the yard at lunchtime, the blue sky overhead. The teachers are softer, more forgiving; they aren't so hard-ass if someone forgets his social-studies homework or screws up on a quiz. His mother tries to pick him up when she can so he doesn't have to take the bus, and it seems every other day she's got a new look, depending on the audition she's been sent on. One day it's vampy, with fake silver chains looped at her hips, and another it's just simple and girlish, with a blue dress and flat sandals. The color of her hair is still shocking against her skin, and when she tips her head toward the sun, he can see the high arches of her cheeks, her narrow collarbone. "That's your sister?" this guy Carlos asks him one afternoon. Today she's wearing white cropped pants and a halter, showing off her long brown arms. "Man, she looks like she could go here."

"Yeah."

"You guys party and stuff together?"

He shakes his head. "Nah. My sister's not like that. She's strict."

"Yeah, but *still*."

Sandi drives across town, where she has an audition, and this time, she lets him sit in the waiting room and read the magazines. Once again he's stuck with stuff he couldn't care less about: *Variety* and *Entertainment Weekly*. A parade of young women goes by as he's waiting. Most of them he guesses to be just a few years older than he is: their hipbones sticking out of their jeans, their footsteps a little skittish. Definitely not the kind of girls he'd want to go out with. The audition is for a long-distance phone commercial. Those are great for the "ethnically ambiguous," as Larry puts it. They always want some Asian or black family calling a grandmother in Bangkok or Mississippi. Very "We Are the World," very heartwarmingly global. When the guy with the clipboard comes out to call in the next person, his glance shifts to Victor.

"Who's he?" he asks.

Victor gets a wobbly feeling in his stomach. "I'm—"

"He's with me," his mother puts in. "My little brother. I hope it's okay—"

"He model?" The clipboard guy says it so fast Victor doesn't understand, and so the man says it again, impatiently. "Model. Act. You done any ads before? You got a tear sheet?"

His mother rises, smoothes her pants. "Not really."

The guy jabs his clipboard at Victor. "You want to give it a try?"

Victor looks down at his shoes. They're the new ones his mother bought for him. His ankles look too thin.

Victor and Sandi are called into the large room, where a bunch of people are sitting around a table. Victor is supposed to sit on a folding chair. The lights slide down warm on his face and neck.

"It's just what we were looking for, only they came together."

"This is a brother-and-sister thing." A woman laughs. "He's

stuck at home with the 'rents and the sister is calling from her first apartment in New York. You get it?"

They hand them the script. It's easy: Victor, kid brother, is jealous and sullen; he's been left in a boring suburban house, while his older sister has a new job and friends. But then at the end, she says something about how the ice cream doesn't taste the same in New York, and that's because they always used to have it together. Very reach-across-the-wires goopy-sweet, but when Victor and Sandi read the lines out loud, he can tell, right away, that they like it. Maybe because he and his mother have played characters before, in real life, invented new ones every time they've moved, told the landlord a different story about why they have to break the lease, or why some of Sandi's papers bear a different name. They go through the script again, and by the time they walk out of there, he knows for sure: They've got the job.

And so Victor Brown the Actor, Sandi Brown's kid brother, is born. Larry sends him for photos, too, and he spends a whole day putting on all kinds of outfits and having the stylist muss daubs of sticky gel in his hair, getting his nails trimmed by a Russian girl with a tattoo flaming around her shoulder. It drives him crazy, all this fidgeting, and he just wants to bolt from the room and go for a swim or a walk on the boardwalk.

"I see a sitcom, baby," Larry exclaims. "They're gonna write one around you two."

"God, I hope not." Sandi sighs when they're done with the photo shoot and driving home, after picking up groceries. The bottles of beer she's bought clink against one another every time she rounds a corner.

"But why do we have to be a brother and sister for real?" Victor asks. "This is the movies. TV. Why can't we just play a brother and sister?"

She shrugs. "I don't know. But now that we've started, we can't stop."

And it does start. Faster than he could ever imagine. Victor goes on auditions, half of them with his mother, half without. At school, those soft and forgiving teachers learn he's one of those—a child actor—and they figure out how to do his assignments and give him flexible deadlines. Victor doesn't feel like an actor. He feels as if Victor from Brooklyn is a smudge of memory, fading to nothing, especially when Sandi announces Friday evening that she wants to dye his hair.

"Ma!"

"Victor, please. Larry says it will make a great sell. I'll do it myself."

"But, Ma, I want to—"

"What?"

His heart beats, wildly. He wants to say: *I want to take a girl out, regularlike. I want to sit in the movies and feel her thigh press against mine.*

Instead they get in the car and drive to her salon in Santa Monica, where she sweeps the nylon smock over his shoulders and tilts his head back into a little basin, tenderly massaging his hair with shampoo. She takes forever to do the color: brushing the thick mud all over his skull, expertly squeezing out the excess from his sodden curls. He's never seen her in action as a hairdresser, and he's impressed: She attacks it with the same vigor and belief as she does every one of her crazy schemes. She'll make something happen, a new look, a new face, a new cut, a new life. Then he's got his head tipped into the basin again, and she's gently rinsing, and she leads him by the hand to the chair, rubbing the towel hard before she undrapes.

He stares, a little in shock. His cropped halo of curls is now the exact color of his mother's. He sees the two of them in the mirror: the same brassy skin and hair the color of a camel-hair coat, only brighter. Rivulets of wetness dribble down his brow and cheeks, and when he goes to wipe them away, he realizes they're tears, hot and salty.

After that, they land some more gigs: Sandi and Victor Brown, the golden-haired brother–sister team. They pose for a brandy ad, where his mother is in a white sleeveless dress, and he's in a white suit, too young to drink of course, but the creative director explains he gives an impression of "innocence" to the liquor. They do a Ralph Lauren spread, one of those scenes on some fake prairie grass, where they're clad in turquoise-stone belts and moccasins, and their "mother" is a strong-faced Native American lady, whose knuckled brown hands rest on their shoulders. Ralph is looking to "branch," they were told, sell not just the WASPy dream. That ad leads to more such dreams—they sell a Caribbean cruise and a Mercedes car and a new nougat chocolate bar. They're set up with all kinds of "parents": a distinguished, professorial, Spanish-looking man extolling the cocoa extract in the chocolate bar; two sharp-faced, silver-haired, and tanned people who lean with them on the hood of the Mercedes while the wind machine blows so hard, Victor's eyeballs feel grazed and dry.

Sandi learns that being Victor's older sister has its advantages. All the things that people took for granted when she was a single mother—shuttling him to doctors' appointments, checking on his homework, doing the grocery shopping—now are endearing, amazing, heroic, even; the sign of a twenty-five-year-old with real grit and strength. She has Larry send her on auditions for hard-scrabble, suffering women who beat all the odds, Lifetime TV roles about some woman who has survived a creepy abusive uncle and is taking care of her orphaned brood while looking great in Laura Ashley dresses.

When Victor limps out of bed every morning, a stranger with yellow hair peers groggily at him. His eyes are puffy—from posing under too many lights. A stiffness comes over him. It's like when his mother did his hair: the cold slime of dye mixture and slow baking after, under a heat lamp, until he felt as if he'd been covered in a thick new skin. Now it's as if he's been cast in a clay mold that will crack if he moves too fast. His collars itch; his pants are creased too sharply; the words fall from his lips, false and wooden. He can't seem to have a natural conversation with anyone at school, making him raw and miserable on the inside.

They've got a bit of money, with some of the checks coming in, though his mother still cuts hair three days a week at a salon in Santa Monica. Sandi has put photos of them all over the apartment—propped up on the stackable bookcase, on the windowsills, in the kitchen, by the coffee machine. Which is why, when his friend Carlos wants to come over and hang—"You've got a swimming pool, man"—he says no.

"Why not?" Sandi asks. "You know your friends are perfectly welcome."

Victor squirms. She sounds different when they're alone—she's back to being a mother, with that hectoring tension in her voice, like a thick cabled wire. "I dunno. What would we do here?"

"Play music. Go to the pool. Talk." She slaps her hands against her thighs. "Please, Victor. Don't act so strange! This is a home!"

And so he agrees, the next day, to have Carlos come over, and at the last minute, Carlos asks if his sister can come, too—Maria, who's in ninth grade and really likes to swim. The instant Maria shows up with her books pressed against her chest, he realizes what this is about: She has a crush on him. They're in some class together, an elective—art history. She sits in the back and wears collared shirts and skirts that fall below the knee. He's almost relieved, as it reminds him of the old days, back in Brooklyn, when he and Cecilia almost had something going.

"You guys always live in L.A.?" Victor asks.

Carlos nods. "Forever. My whole family's here. All my father's brothers. They come over our house, and it's like the windows are busting out of the walls."

Victor feels a pang, like a knife making a swift pass across his chest. He wishes he knew more about family—cousins, uncles, meddling aunts. He and Sandi are often more like oddball companions, trying out guises. He asks Carlos and Maria a lot of questions, enviously eating up every detail: how they've lived in the same house for years and their grandmother lives across the yard and brings them rice and meat dishes kept warm with a towel. He notices now, as they're waiting for his mother to pull up in the dented Honda, that Maria has the tiniest ears, with round gold studs in her lobes. He has an image, suddenly, of a good confirmation girl in her ruffly lace, her big brother Carlos soberly guiding her toward the church aisle. This is a real brother–sister, he thinks. They look out for each other.

When Sandi pulls up, she's wearing her chic sunglasses and a dazzling gold tank top that looks like fish scales, shimmering and catching in the sun. She's just come from the gym, and her skin is oiled and fresh. He can see Maria's mouth open in surprise. Victor unhappily gets in beside his mother, and the other two slide in the back.

Sandi doesn't get out with them at the apartment house. "You kids, do what you want. There's plenty of soda in the fridge."

"Where are you going?" He's relieved, actually, that she won't be around: With that crazy gold top and her hair and her bronzed arms, she's dazzling and blotting everything out—especially poor Maria, who's hunched against the left rear door, fiddling with her notebook.

"Appointment, luvie." She taps his nose. "Larry and I are going to talk about a big one." Then she's gone.

They change in the little cabana and splash around in the pool. Victor has brought down some Cokes and chips, and after they're done swimming, they stretch out on the lounge chairs, feeling the water bead and dry on their skin. Maria looks pretty good in a bathing suit—she's short and compact, her legs strong. She's not such a priss, either; they run through all the teachers at school, and she and Carlos give him their nicknames for everyone. Mr. Don't-Forget-I-Was-the-Coolest-Dashiki-Brother-in-the-Sixties, who teaches American history. Mrs. I-Am-the-World, the cheery English teacher who encourages them to trade ethnic recipes and always say hello in their native languages.

"Mrs. Flag-Lady," Carlos cracks, about the principal, a formal woman who stands by the door doing a meet-and-greet every morning.

"Tell him about the time you ran into her in the supermarket," Maria adds.

"Oh, yeah. She was with her kid. About our age. And she was slapping him. I mean really slapping him. I turned the corner, and she said to me—"

"Do you have a hallway pass?" Maria chimes in.

"No, no. She was really embarrassed."

They all laugh, and Victor realizes that this is the first time he's felt normal since they've come to California. He says things—silly things—without thinking about it. He even does a few of his cartwheels across the wet patio for Maria, who laughs, hard. Emboldened, when Carlos is in for another swim, he rolls over and asks, "So what do you do on Friday nights?"

A smile flickers across her face. "Stuff. Hang with my girl-friends."

"Maybe we could hang sometime, too."

"Sure." He knows she's pleased because there's a deep flush starting up her neck and over her cheeks.

He's about to say something else, when a voice floats toward them, and he turns to see his mother standing by the gate. "Hey! Come on, kids! I've got lots of goodies!" She's got a big flowery bag on her shoulder, and she's still wearing her sunglasses. Maria pulls back a little; the conversation between them seems to shrink and vanish in the air.

They go upstairs and take turns showering in the bathroom—when Victor emerges, he sees Maria tilting one of the photographs off the sill. It gives Victor a slightly queasy feeling, as if two parts of his life are banging together. "You model?" she asks.

He shrugs. His mother is humming in the kitchen, bringing out a baguette and cold cuts and cheese. "A little." Maria's holding up the picture of them posing for Ralph Lauren, and he can see her brow pucker, as if she's perplexed. Her hair is still wet and is sprinkling her neck and back—he wishes, with a sudden tenderness, that he could wipe them dry.

"Hey kids!" Sandi claps her hands enthusiastically.

"How did you get started—like that?" Maria asks. There's

another photo of them, twined around each other, propped by the salt- and pepper-shakers.

Sandi laughs nervously and stretches an arm around Victor. "It was just a silly freak thing. Victor came with me to an audition. And they loved him. Loved us, together. So we thought—" She shrugs. "Why not? We have been together all these years. Like a really tight team." She ruffles Victor's hair. "Isn't it beautiful? I did it myself."

Victor wants to push his mother off him, make her go away for good.

She starts yanking him up from the chair. "Come, *mi querido*. Let's show them. Our telephone ad." She juts out her hip.

"Ma . . . Sandi, no!"

"Go ahead!" Carlos laughs.

Sandi hurries into the living room and pops the tape into the player. It's only three minutes, but the whole time, Victor is burning with humiliation. He keeps trying to read Maria's face, to see if she likes it, but he can't tell. She has this studied look, as if she can't figure out what's going on here, exactly.

"So what do you think?" Sandi asks, draping her arm around Victor.

"Very cool," Carlos enthuses.

"My baby brother. He's a natural."

Victor pries off Sandi's arm—it's a bar between him and Maria. He can see that Sandi is making Maria feel small and plain—his mother is taking up too much space in the apartment; she shimmers like a glamorous sea creature, while Maria squirms on her seat, can't seem to get comfortable.

"So what about Friday?" he asks, once dinner is finished, and they're heading for the door.

Maria tucks her hair behind her ear. It's still a little wet, and there are droplets hanging from her lobe. "You probably get to go to clubs and meet famous people with your sister," she says.

"Not really."

She gives him a skeptical look. He feels as if he, too, has turned into an alien creature, different from them.

"Maybe she's right, Victor," Sandi calls from the kitchen. "We do have a big audition. And we have to practice."

He hates this. Because she's his mother, he can't cross her—he was raised to be polite, especially in front of guests. But she's also acting like his big sister, twisting him around her finger. By the time the door shuts, Victor knows he and Maria are not going out, not this Friday, maybe not ever.

Later Sandi hands him the script—he plays, once again, the sullen younger brother of a twenty-two-year-old who's being stalked by her ex-boyfriend. They practice every night, and even when he's sitting in classes, he can hear the dialogue, ringing in his head: *Leave my sister alone. Don't come here again, dude. I'll put a knife in you if I see you near her again.*

He tries to spend some time with Carlos and Maria, but there's something awkward between them now. The stiffness has returned; he sounds fake, a boss booming his questions—How-are-you-what-have-you-been-up-to? And she's shy, blushing and stammering. That makes him sore and confused, and then sore all over again. They look at him through different eyes, he thinks. Not only is he a child actor, but he's got this thing with his sister. They don't want to get inside that.

Angry, he works out longer, with even tougher routines. The muscles in his arms, his chest, are hard as stone. His shirts pull tight under his armpits. He's starting to think that maybe the girls at school think he's gay. But he doesn't know what else to do. Everything makes him feel even more apart.

The afternoon before the audition, Victor is digging through his closet, looking for his basketball, when he comes upon an envelope of old snapshots. There they are, he and Sandi, squinting into the sun on a Miami beach. He's eight years old with skinny legs and dirty knees, and she's holding him tight, kissing him on the cheek. There's another of him—just four—riding a tricycle in a wizard cap and one-piece pajamas. He can almost hear his mother, proudly coaxing him down the hall.

Then he remembers how that was the Christmas she announced they were moving, and how he was terrified—of their new city with its new big boulevards, of the strange woman who was his mother and had a strange new name. It happened again and again, and each time there was the same corkscrew of fear that nothing would ever stay still. And this time is worse, he realizes. Because now it is not just her who's changing—it's him, too.

When Sandi comes home, she finds Victor curled up in bed, crying silently into the pillow. She drops down beside him. "Oh, baby, no."

"Mama." His cheeks are wet. "This is too weird. I can't do it."

"I promise, once my career is really launched, all of this will be over. They won't care about this brother–sister thing. It's just a gimmick."

"I want my life, Ma. I want to go back to the way it was."

She strokes his head, his ears, so softly he almost drifts to sleep. "*Mi querido.* My baby. It will be all right. It will. Just give me this. Please."

Victor closes his eyes. His mother's fingertips are light, soothing. Exhausted, he imagines himself inside the tender whorl of memory; he's in one of those photographs, still so young, so trusting.

Why, oh why, did he know they would get the parts? He knew it the minute they walked down the carpeted corridor after the audition, into the parking lot; he knew it that night when Larry called, nervous and excited; and he knew it the next day when he woke, full of loathing, an acidy taste coating his mouth. He knows they got the movie because he didn't want it. The more he snapped out his lines and hunched his shoulders—the more they loved it. He tried—in every possible way—to signal that he couldn't possibly be her brother. Afterward, the casting director stood with him next to the Coke machine and asked how he felt about going up to Vancouver for a few weeks.

I feel like it's a waste, he wanted to say. *Someone else wants this more than me.* Instead he shrugged and said, "I guess."

And sure enough, Sandi comes bursting through the door a few days later and throws her arms around his neck, silent, astonished. They breathe into each other, her heart fluttering against his chest; his hands clumsy on her back. It grinds into him in tiny bitter bits, and he thinks: It won't end. She won't stop the lie.

The next few days are a flurry of arrangements: conference calls, a release from school, finding a tutor for him on the set. A new version of the script, delivered by messenger, in a glossy black cover.

The next time he sees Carlos and Maria together, outside the school, they're friendly to him, but it's a cold-friendly, like he's already a star, a person who lives outside their orbit. When Carlos saunters away to greet another friend, Victor musters up his nerve and asks Maria, "So. What about this Friday?"

Her mouth goes into a pout. "What about it?"

"You want to hang?"

Her eyes are on her brother's back. "Don't you have other things to do?"

"Not really."

Just then his mother pulls up in the Honda, swings open the door. She's wearing a white miniskirt and a flesh-colored tank top. She looks practically nude. "Come on, hon! I have to get to the salon in an hour!"

Victor doesn't move. He looks at Maria, and just wishes he could press his fingertips into her arm, feel the soft dent of her skin.

That afternoon Victor lies in the bedroom with the shades drawn, sealing the room in shadows. He imagines Maria lying next to him, his hands running up her thighs. His whole body aches. He doesn't even go downstairs to swim. He just wants to stay here, in the dark, unseen, unmoving. Never again to be under those hot lights or in some stupid glossy ad. He feels as if his skin will catch on fire if he has to live this crazy lie one more day.

When the phone rings he almost doesn't answer, but then he doesn't want his mother yelling at him later. It's some girl named Valerie, a stylist, who wants him to come in and try on clothes. They're sending a car in ten minutes.

She meets him at the back of the studio lot and takes him down a long hallway into a room stuffed with clothes. Valerie's hair is chopped up into black and rust-colored spikes; a silver hoop glints in her belly button. He tries on outfits, and they start to laugh—at the dorky orange T-shirt and the carpenter pants that barely squeeze around his hips. She's supposed to make notes on a clipboard, but soon she's just writing in loopy letters: *God Help Us, Don't Put Him on Prime Time.*

He doesn't really like Valerie—she strikes him as spoiled and gossipy: She tells him about how the director is coming out of rehab and the costume designer got fired from her last job for filching all the clothes and selling them on eBay. Still, when they're finished and she asks him, "You want to smoke?" he nods yes.

She lights up the joint, the two of them crouched on the linoleum floor, their knees drawn up, clothes strewn all around them. "How'd you get this job?" he asks her.

Her nostrils, pale and thin as feathers, flare as she sucks on the joint. "My dad. He's in the business. Executive producer on this."

"That's the way it is, huh?" Victor asks. "Connections. Through relatives."

She shrugs. "Like with you and your sister. Ever hear of Donny and Marie Osmond? My dad has their records." She nudges him hard, in the ribs, passes the joint, and tells him about the Osmonds.

For some reason, he finds this hysterically funny—he and his mother dressed up in some sky-blue outfit with perfectly white teeth, acoustic guitars. That's where they're headed. This isn't some temporary gig, a little stop on the way to Sandi's career. This is forever, emblazoned on billboards, in *TV Guide*s, on movie credits. Sandi has stolen his future, his name beside someone else's. Anything could happen, and the ceiling seems to fly up, and he's laughing so hard, it's as if his ribs will splinter. Then he remembers Maria, and how she gave him that odd look earlier today, and hot tears squeeze out the sides of his eyes.

"You know," he gasps, taking another toke. "My sister. She's not my sister. She's my mom."

Valerie turns to him, eyes wide. "You serious?"

He nods. The air seems to pulse around him, breaking up into tiny, electric pricks.

"No shit. It was just something we made up. And it worked."

She lets out a squeal, slaps her hand on his knee. "That's the weirdest thing I've ever heard!"

Groggy, he stumbles outside, amazed by the deep fuchsia bleeding across the sky, the knifelike silhouettes of palm trees. At home, he falls asleep in his bedroom with his clothes on, feeling a little soiled, as if there's ash and dirt in his mouth.

Victor is on Venice beach, pushing his feet into the cold gray sand, letting the sun's weak rays settle into his skin. It feels good being here: the skateboarders, the two gay guys with their great tans and golden retriever, the straight couple pushing a jogging stroller. Ever since he smoked with Valerie two days ago, he's changed; his thoughts are loose and limber. He isn't watching himself so much, wondering if he's doing or saying the right thing.

Stretching out, he finds himself thinking about his father with a sudden sharpness, like a hunger. He doesn't often think about his father. But now it's as if he can feel and see their story, the one that's stamped on them for life: the stranger who walked through the glass doors into the air-conditioned shop, the light growing white and hard around him, like sculpted marble. His father's skin was the color of amber, and his hair was a tight halo of curls. His mother laid out tie after tie on the counter, stripes, diamond patterns, solids, and he liked every single one, spending hundreds of dollars, all cash. It went on for months, this dizzying dream, and every time they undressed and their skins touched, it was as if she knew they would make a child; there was an electrical zap between them, a melding of cells and blood.

That's what his life has always been, to enter his mother's tale, to take on whatever role was given him. But he doesn't want that anymore. He just wants to lie on the warm sand, feel the sun's rays on his lids, making him groggy and slow. To be here. Now. Not pretending. Not making anything up.

A slight shadow falls across his lap. When he turns, he's surprised. His mother's face looks as if it's been crumpled on one side. "I don't get it. They put the gig on hold. No explanation." She takes a breath and adds, "Larry's being strange, too. He doesn't answer my calls."

Victor feels a pang as she drops down beside him. But he also feels better already—lighter, freer, even happy to be in California and to try again. He takes his mother into his strong, sure arms. She leans into him and starts to cry. "Oh, Vic." This is what endures, he thinks: She's family, all in one person: his mother, his sister, his fellow traveler in this life of theirs, each of them needing the other. This is the way it's always been, this chemical zap between them, his molecules and hers, hair, eyes, mouth, and neck. From now on, he'll take care of her, he tells himself as they sit watching the waves break on the shore.

by ●
Evelyn
Coleman

At seventeen, I have to remake myself every single day.

Weekdays, I am a student, waking up at 6:00 A.M., scrounging around until I find something dorky to wear, eating crunchy sugar-packed cereal, and then catching a city bus to school.

"Jamillah, you're late."

"I'm sorry, Miss Pritchard, the bus broke down, the street-lights were busted, the driver passed out, flat tire, engine blew up, robbed, mugged, and that's why I'm late."

"Jamillah, can you sit up, please."

"Yes, Mr. Dorn, I'm sorry, didn't sleep last night, people in a fight, Mama drunk, friends held up, police raid, drug bust, rape next door, is why I'm laying my head down."

"Jamillah, what is that smell? Have you been drinking alcohol?"

"No, Miss Cruise. I spilled Listerine, bottle of perfume broke, Mama wore my clothes, brother squirted me with water gun filled with something, bum ran into me on my way to school, is why I'm smelling like this."

"Jamillah, why didn't you finish this test?"

Stare.

"Jamillah, do you hear me talking to you?"

Stare.

"Jamillah, if you keep this up, there is no way you're going to qualify for a scholarship."

"Yes, ma'am."

Friday night, I'm an exotic dancer. That means I dress up, smear on heavy eyeliner, even heavier makeup, dark red lipstick, put on my mama's push-up bra and matching top, a tight, tight, leather skirt, ankle strap, high-heeled shoes, and strut my stuff—that way I look older than I am. Catch the train—cringe when men whistle at me. Damn perverts! At the club, fake ID, no problem—don't even need it unless cops show up. Friday—no raids, so they say. I don't drink much, just down about three wine coolers, okay, most times six, my magic number.

Put on my uniform that the club makes me pay for out of my money—sleek black dress, tiger-print boa, long black gloves, and underneath, two tiger's eyes where my tits are and a furry orange-and-black G-string that sports a cat's tail on the back to go along with my stage name, Miss Puss. Then I dance till the sweat rolls off me in perfumed drops, while I'm taking off my uniform, slowly, slowly, real slow. I don't have to worry about my hair kinking up 'cause I got a weave—a blond one. G-string stays on so I have a place to get paid.

I am up onstage, grab the pole, do the nasty with it, swing my ass 'round and 'round. Squeeze my breasts together to snatch some of the money from the grubby hands. Stick my tongue out, pretend to lick ice cream, all the time my eyes closed. Some nights I think I'll actually fall off the stage. Serve me right.

When it's all said and done, put my clothes back on, strap up my shoes, stagger back on the train, enter huge room, then flop on cot, slip most of the money, except a few dollars, into my spot.

The next day, Saturday, I hop up early, put on my other uniform, turtleneck sweater, long ankle skirt, no earrings, no makeup, and head to church; choir practice.

"Jamillah, I want you to sing the solo today."

"Heifer, she gets all the solos."

"No, she doesn't, Phyllis. Jamillah sing."

Underbreath: "Witch with a *B*."

"Phyllis, shut up so Jamillah can sing."

Outside church doors.

"Jamillah, you think you all that. Well, you ain't."

"Phyllis, say another damn word to me, and I'll stomp your ass right here."

"Ain't nobody scared of you, Jamillah."

"You better be. Now back off."

"Come on, Phyllis, leave that hoing-ass Jamillah alone. At least you ain't dancing naked on no stage."

"You got that right, Kiki. Talking 'bout going to hell . . . Bitch, you on your way."

Me—walking, crying, shaking with fury. Tired of this bull. Tired of it all. Seventeen more years of this shit and I'll be like her.

"Jamillah, where the hell have you been? You know damn well I wanted you to keep the kids this morning while I look for a job."

Keep the kids? What a laugh; half the time she don't know where they at. She doing this now, talking all loud, 'cause the shelter's warned her they're going to call the authorities if she keeps going off for days at a time. I ask her, "How you gon' find a job on Saturday?"

"That's my damn business. You got any money?"

"No, Mama, I don't—have—any—money," I say, watching her prancing like some racehorse getting ready to run.

"What about the money in the jar?"

Once a week, I put fifty one-dollar bills in a jar under the bed in the box of shoes so that I can buy the kids candy or ice cream on the weekends, or pay for something for school for me or them.

"Don't touch it," I say, offering her the meanest look I got. "I ain't playing, Mama."

She glares back, but doesn't make her move. Since I'm older now and taller, she doesn't always know how to take me. She says, "Shit," and heads out the door.

I wipe the sweat from my face. I can remember when she'd of busted my mouth open.

I grab some clothes, head to the bathroom. Wash up in the sink. Put on jeans and a T-shirt that says *Women Rock*. Come back out.

"Jamillah, can you help me with my homework?"

"Jamillah, Chucky is hurting me."

"Jamillah, can I ask that man for candy?"

"Jamillah."

"Jamillah."

"Jamillah, can I go to the store?"

"Jamillah, how many more days we got?"

Sitting on my cot, I look up. Hmm. "Bring me that calendar, Peaches. Chucky, let go of Brian before you hurt him for real. Brian, sit your ass down. Cookie, you better not take your fast self over there bothering that man. How many times I got to tell you about that. Celia, come sit by me and I'll help you as soon as I check out this calendar."

I stare. We have one more week of school. And here, two more days—that's it. We got two more days. Shelters have a long waiting list of people trying to get a few days. We've been here three months; supposed to be enough time for Mama to find a job or a more permanent place for us, an example of the shelter's fantasies.

Celia says, "You gon' help me, Jamillah?"

I look over her paper again. "Celia, you take away five right here. See that minus, that means to subtract."

"What do *subtract* mean, Jamillah?"

"Chucky, my God, you're in the fourth grade. You don't know what *subtract* means?"

"I know, Jamillah. Chucky know, too. He just playing, ain't you, Chucky?"

"I ain't playing, Brian. Just 'cause we twins don't mean I know what you know, stupid. What is it, Jamillah?"

I sigh a big, long sigh. Everybody in this joint should know about subtraction. Check out the room. It's a huge room with cots every few feet, little warped white plastic table between each one for your toothbrush and shit. The cots are so close to the floor, if you sit on one, your knees are at your chin. Some of the old people have to be pulled up out of bed each morning.

On the side where we are, a few metal tables line the wall near a fridge. They moved this one out here because they didn't want anyone in the kitchen without supervision. The fridge usually has some water, cheese, crackers, and a few pieces of fruit in it. Lately, they put the sugar for the coffee inside on account of the roaches.

There's one picture on the wall of Jesus holding a heart with blood dripping out of it. Reminds me of the horror movie I'm living. Nothing else. The room is bare, grayish, and hot. The building's air-conditioned, but five giant-size fans clank, like cars with bad motors, to save on electricity. The cots are old, the sheets on them dingy and some ripped. A few cots have army blankets, despite the fact that it's hot and stinks like a homeless man's socks. Of course, in this joint it probably *is* a homeless man's socks stinking.

"Hmm. Take away. Okay, it's like this," I finally say. "Cookie, give me that apple, off that table over there."

"But it don't belong to us, Jamillah. That woman will be mad at me."

The old woman is sitting down with a plate of cheese and crackers. The apple is near her plate, her dessert.

"Get it anyway," I say. "Don't worry, just run over there and snatch it, then run back over here to me. Quick now!" The woman is new. If you're not a family, you only get to stay a few days before you rotate out. It don't matter that she new, since Mama makes it hard for us to get to know anyone in the shelters. She's always picking fights or stealing something. The shelters can't prove she took it, but the people know.

"Jamillah, let me do it."

"No, Chucky, you just wait."

I watch Cookie snatch the apple and run. She drops it. It rolls away; she grabs it quickly and makes it back to me, just as the woman's hands grip her collar.

"Turn her the hell a loose," I say to the woman.

"But she took my apple," she says, panting, her gray hair melting down into her face. Bending over, holding her arthritic kneepads.

"Here," I say, snatching the apple from Cookie's pudgy fingers. "Take it away."

"I get it," Chucky says.

I look at him. "Do you?"

The woman says, "What the . . . ?"

I shrug. "I'm trying to teach them subtraction."

"Oh," she says. "All right, but you best be teaching addition."

I shake my head. She's right. Subtraction is going to be what they know most.

Sunday morning, I wake up early, put on my uniform, same one I had on Saturday. I only have one turtleneck and one ankle-length skirt. The kids are gone on a "Sunday school" bus. Every Sunday, a bus from some church comes early to take all the little kids—probably just to fill up their classes, since the churches don't come back on no routine or nothing.

I check my watch. It's 10:20. I bend down like I'm rubbing my shoe clean. I glance around hoping no one sees me. This is the best time to handle your business, since the shelter makes everyone leave by 10:30 to go to church. Most don't go, but they got to get out anyway. By now, only a few stragglers remain.

I've punctured a hole in the bottom of the cot mattress. It's a risk to keep my bling here, because when nobody's much watching, people check out the mattresses for stashes just like this. I rotate mine from somewhere on my body to the mattress every six days. I always take it with me on Sundays, though. So far, I've been lucky.

I have two thousand dollars in tips for four months of dancing. I changed it into hundreds at the bank. Well, not exactly a real bank, since I had to pay. I paid my boss to change it into hundred-dollar bills; cost me a ten for every hundred. I have never had this much money. Actually, I have never *seen* this much money. I doubt my mama's seen this much at one time. I pop it from the mattress, and with my head still scoping the room, I stick the cash inside the top of the bands of my skirt and panties in one smooth move.

I hop up and head for the bathroom. I feel the wad silking next to my skin as I walk, tugging and pulling up against the hairs as it works its way downward. I know the money is dirty, but I don't care. It was just as dirty when they stuffed it inside my G-string. I'll never dance again, at least not that way. Water can't wash that dirt away. In the bathroom, I hunker down in one of the three stalls. None of them have doors on them. Privacy is something you don't get much of in most shelters, not even to shit.

I flatten the money, fold it, and wrap toilet tissue around it a few times. The tissue is stiffer than newspaper. I use a big safety pin to keep the tissue in place. I pray that it won't slip out. Pants would be better, but I don't see nobody at this church wearing pants.

I almost run all the way to church. I quickly slip on my choir robe and join the procession. When it's time, I sing the solo, "Give Me a Clean Heart." I choke up a few times, but don't mess up the key. I hear the people sniffling, shouting out, "Yes, Lord. Help me, Jesus."

I keep my eyes shut, praying over and over as I sing "Give Me a Clean Heart."

After church, I say to the preacher, "Do you think that God will give us a clean heart if we pray for it? I mean, no matter what we've done? How mean we've been? The kind of sins we've done?"

The preacher stands very still for a minute. I can hear his heart beat. Everything is like in a vacuum-sealed pack. Finally he says, "No, Jamillah."

I turn to walk away. Tears burn my eyes. Another wasted prayer. It's too late for me. No more makeovers.

"Jamillah," he says, "you already have one."

I look back. "One what?"

"A clean heart," he says, smiling.

I don't believe him, but I smile back.

When I get back, Mama is waiting. "Jamillah, I'm going out for a bit. You got any money?"

"No, ma'am. Mama. You know we only have one more day before we have to get out, right?"

"Damn shelters," she says. "Motherfuckers always got some goddamn stupid-ass rules. We'll talk about what we gon' do when I get back. You just watch them kids. I took the treat money out the jar. Them younguns' teeth already rott'n; they don't need no sweets."

"Yeah, whatever," I say, staring at her back. There's no arguing with the logic of a drug addict. She's got on all leopard-skin-looking shit. Nose running. I know where she's headed. So do the other kids. I hug them close to me and decide—I've had it.

I wash my hair in one of four bathroom sinks. All of them so rusty, they look like they've been painted orange. It takes forever because the sink is about the size of a basketball. I have to fill a cup with water a thousand times to rinse the suds out. I cut my weave out with some nail scissors. Today is the day.

Celia, who always sticks to me like glue, is watching, alarm on her face. "What you doing, Jamillah? I like your long hair."

"It was only mine 'cause I paid for it. I want natural now."

When I come out of the bathroom, the kids all gather around. "Why you chop your hair off like that, Jamillah?"

"I'm changing myself. In fact, y'all know what?"

"What, Jamillah," they say, "what?"

"I'm going to teach y'all addition today."

"For real," Chucky says, grinning. "I caught on to that subtraction stuff. You a good teacher, Jamillah."

"Yeah, you the best teacher," Cookie and Celia say.

"Yeah, you the bomb, Jamillah," Brian and Peaches sing together.

The old woman comes over.

Cookie runs behind me. "Don't let her get me, Jamillah."

"I won't," I say. "What you want? I gave you the apple back."

"I know," she says. "Here, this will help you when you ready to teach them younguns some addition."

She places a man's dingy handkerchief in my hand.

"What is it?"

"Open it later," she says. "You'll see."

"Thank you," I say, wondering if she's being funny and it's an apple core or something. I look at the kids. They're all staring at me.

"I don't have much time," I say. "We're leaving today, kids. Get your shit."

"What about Mama, Jamillah?"

"Don't worry about Mama, just get your shit. Hurry. We're leaving this shelter, and we're leaving this town."

Cookie says, "But, Jamillah, we don't have to leave until tomorrow. And what about school?"

"Only got a week. You've taken your test. We leaving today," I say, throwing my shit into a black plastic trash bag. "Get all your stuff and put it in these bags. Leave Mama the suitcase."

The kids throw clothes and worn shoes into bags. It's no use folding what's already wrinkled.

While they pack I call the church on the one pay phone. When they're all ready, I pat my panties. "Let's go."

We head for the church. Outside, I wait for the reverend's wife. I open the handkerchief. There's six tightly twisted dollars in it, my lucky number. Somehow this makes me feel hopeful.

Chucky says, "Shit, it's hot out here."

I say, "Kids, no more cursing. Okay. Not from anybody. Not even me."

"We subtracting that?" Celia says.

"I thought it first," Chucky says.

The preacher's wife comes out. We pile into her van. "Where are you and the kids going, Jamillah?" She's taking us to the bus stop. The Trailways.

"Greensboro, North Carolina. Your husband told me once that was a good place to start over. I am going to make myself into someone new. Going to get a place, in a good neighborhood, and go to night school and work in the day. Then I'm going to college."

The kids know my dreams, they all sing, "Yeah, Jamillah is going to college. Jamillah is going to college."

"Do you need any money?" she asks.

"No, ma'am. I have some."

"You're sure about this? Won't your mama have a fit?"

"Only if I'm taking her drugs with me. She don't care."

"What about them?" she says. "Won't they miss your mama?"

"To them, I'm the mama. Our mama has been gone for a very long time."

"Will she give us trouble? Call the cops?"

I laugh. "You're kidding, right?" I see she's not. People just don't get it. They don't understand the life a crack addict leads. It ain't like television. "First off, she don't even know I go to church. Second, she wouldn't call the cops if somebody was beating all of us to death. Cops are like kryptonite to her."

The preacher's wife looks like she'll be crying in a second. She holds out a piece of paper, "Here, here is the name of a friend of mine in Burlington, North Carolina; that's only twenty minutes from Greensboro. She's my old teacher, Annie Saunders. I bet she'll let you stay with her until you get a place. Yes, go there; people will look out for you. She goes to this church, Ebenezer United Church of Christ."

"But you're Baptist?"

"That doesn't matter," she says. "The preacher's name is Reverend Covington. He and his wife are doing marvelous things to help the community."

"Thank you," I say, taking the paper from her manicured fingers.

"Do he know addition, Jamillah?" Chucky says. "I want to learn addition."

"Yes," I say, "Chucky, I'm sure he does. From now on, our life is about addition. Okay. And I want you to say, 'Does he know addition?'"

"Okay, Jamillah," Chucky says.

"Do that mean we gon' be adding stuff?"

"Yes, Celia. Good stuff, though. No bad stuff. And say, *are* we adding stuff? Not gon' be adding, okay?" I squeeze my eyes shut. Lay my head back. I don't say it, but we're subtracting Mama. *We have to.*

At the terminal, we all hop out of the van. We're in the back of the station where the passengers load.

"All aboard," a man says to a line of people. "Got your tickets?"

"Come on," I say. "We've got to go inside and buy our tickets."

The preacher's wife gives us a hug good-bye. She's about to break down, so she heads back to her van. Good thing. I don't want the kids to see her sadness.

We stand in line. I straighten my shoulders as we inch closer in the line to the window. I pat down my new Afro. Put on clear lip gloss. Realize I don't know the preacher's first name or his wife's. I've got to pay more attention to small things like that if I am going to take care of the kids.

I smell alcohol wavering in the air. I wish we could take the plane or even the train—never been on either one—probably wouldn't be so many drunks around. But that would take too much of my money. When I am at the window, the man barely glances at me.

"Next," he says.

I clear my throat. "Sir, good afternoon. I'd like to purchase tickets for one adult and five children."

He looks up. "Sorry, how many again, ma'am?"

"That's six in all," Chucky says. "Right, Jamillah?"

"Jamillah, six is your lucky number," Celia says.

"You're both right," I say, smiling. "Yes, sir, that adds up to six tickets in all."

"Here you are, ma'am," he says, passing me the tickets. "Have a nice day."

I smile. My new makeover is working already.

by
Margaret
Peterson
Haddix

BUTTERFLIES

They think I do not know English, these women in this small room.

"Ooh, she's getting married." One of them sighs, leafing through my papers—the papers I slept with, clutched tight in my hand, all the way across the ocean. "Mar-rr-ried?" she says to me, loud and slow, as if I am a deaf old cow.

I do not answer, not because I don't understand, but because I don't have enough English words in my head to explain. Maybe I'll marry Lev, maybe I won't.

Maybe I don't have enough words in my head in any language to explain, even to myself.

"It's so romantic," another coos. "She's come all the way from"—she peers at my papers—"Smyelostada, wherever that is, all by herself, to marry her beloved."

Lev is not my beloved. We threw clods of dirt at each other when we were ten-year-olds tending sheep together in the high meadow. When he left for America, I did not even say good-bye.

But now he and I are the only ones from my village left alive, and that counts for something.

How much it counts for, I do not know. Enough that he wrote that letter, saying I could come here since I did not have anywhere else to go. But enough that we should marry? Enough that I should sleep in his bed and bear his children and cook his meals and wash his clothes, all the rest of my life? Enough that we could be happy?

Happiness is for rich people to worry about, my papa's voice growls in my memory. I want to argue with that: *But, Papa, in America, everyone is rich. I am in America now. Can I not wonder about happiness? Don't I have that right?*

If Papa were here, he would point out that I am not rich, that I have no money but the few coins left over from my journey. He would say that I am only a girl, and girls have no rights. He would not understand that American word, that American idea that I heard about on the ship, that anyone has any right to anything.

It does not do to argue with dead people in your head.

I have practically forgotten the women in this tiny room, staring at me. One of them fingers a patch on my skirt.

"What will she wear for the wedding?" the woman asks. "These old clothes?"

I'd like to see this woman, with her soft face and her soft hands, sew a better patch. I took tiny stitches, the kind you could go blind over, just the way my mama taught me.

"And with that kerchief?" another woman sneers.

The first woman, the one who touched my skirt, starts to pull the scarf from my head. I grab it from her hands, because I am not going to lose that scarf. I can remember my mama weaving the cloth for it, explaining the pattern of brown and green threads to me. My mama had three treasures: a brooch and a ring and a silver thimble that gleamed in the lamplight when she sewed. But all those are gone, lost in the fire or stolen by the soldiers—one or the other, I do not know which. All I have left of my mama is this scarf.

"Touchy, touchy," the woman says, stepping back. "I wasn't going to hurt you," she says, right to my face.

I stand there clutching my scarf, my heart beating against my chest like a frightened bird. I do not know what power these women have over me, over my life. I thought I was through with all the mazes of rooms and lines on Ellis Island. I thought my papers were stamped *Approved*; I thought Lev had been summoned; I thought I only had to wait and then make one final agonizing choice. But maybe I don't understand English as well as I thought. Maybe those words on my papers don't mean *Approved*. Maybe they just mean *Maybe*. Maybe these women can still decide to send me back to my village, back to the soldiers, back to die.

I look at the sign on the wall behind the women—ELLIS ISLAND LADIES' AID SOCIETY. *Society* is not a word I know, and I am afraid to ask about it. On the ship, they said you could be sent back for being stupid.

"These foreigners all look so frumpy," the woman holding my papers complains. "This girl is only—what? Fifteen?" She glances down, corrects herself. "Sixteen. Sixteen years old, and she dresses like some old grandmother in a rocking chair."

I do not understand what she means. In my village, all the women dressed alike: girls, mothers, grandmothers, even one great-grandmother who held on to life long after any normal person would have died. (Held on, that is, until the soldiers came.) You needed a shawl to keep you warm when the winter wind howled out of the mountains; a shirt that left your arms free for pinning up laundry; a skirt wide enough to let you run after the sheep and loose enough that it would not hike up when you sat on your stool, milking the cows. I am lucky to have boots, too—a luxury, because I pulled them out of the fire after the soldiers left. They were not singed too badly.

These women of the Ladies' Aid Society—whatever that is—are dressed like butterflies. Their dresses shimmer blue and yellow and green; their buttons shine like gems. And their hair is short and bouncy, something I have never before seen on a woman. At first I thought it was just a trick of the eye, and they, like me, had a knot of braids hidden up high, at the crown of their head. But I have been looking at them for some time now, while they've been looking at me, and I see it is no trick: Their hair really does end where their necks begin. That would not be practical, I think, if they were outside tending sheep. Their hair would always blow into their eyes, because it's too short to be pinned back. But nothing about their looks is practical. Their skirts are too short and tight to run or milk cows in; their slipper-shoes would be ruined the first time they shoveled out a horse's stall.

These women have probably never run after sheep or milked cows or shoveled out stalls. They *are* butterflies.

The woman who tried to steal my scarf moves in close again. She stands practically nose to nose with me and asks, "Would you like to look like an American?"

That question is a trap, I think. *Not just look like,* I want to tell this woman. *Be.* I have to become an American because I cannot be a villager anymore; my village is gone. But explaining this difference would be like splitting hairs. I do not trust my English to carry the right meaning.

"An American?" the woman says again, louder and closer to

my face. I can smell her perfume, which is frilly and flowery. Lilac or lilies of the valley, maybe—I cannot tell the difference because ever since I left my village, something has been wrong with my nose. Every scent seems to come to me through smoke. "American like us?" she says, pointing at herself and her two butterfly friends.

I nod, because what if I say no and they decide to send me back?

"Wonderful!" the woman with the papers says, clapping her hands together like a delighted child. "With her coloring, don't you think she'd look lovely in mauve?"

"Oh, something lighter than that," the standing-too-close woman says. "Rose, maybe."

They chirp and chatter and twitter around me. From a trunk in the corner of the room, they bring out dresses and skirts and slippers and even undergarments, which makes me blush. Surely they don't expect—?

They point to a screen blocking off one side of the room. I stand behind it, fumbling with unfamiliar buttonholes, unnecessary loops of cloth in odd places. Soon these women will realize I have no money to pay for new clothes; in the meantime, I do not mind playing dress-up, as if they are little girls and I'm their doll.

I step out from behind the curtain and they *ooh* and *aah*.

"I'll dispose of those for you," Blue Dress says, reaching for my old clothes. I clutch them tighter, thinking of the horror of being left naked when they find out I can't pay.

"I keep," I say. "Mine."

"So she has a voice after all!" Green Dress laughs.

"Oh, leave her alone, Iris," Yellow Dress says. She lowers her voice, as though that's enough to keep me from hearing. "Sometimes you have to indulge them a little. These foreigners can be so superstitious."

"We're not done yet," Blue Dress says. "Come along!"

She leads me into another room full of chairs.

"Your turn, George," Blue Dress says to a thin, bald man standing behind one of them.

"Yes, ma'am," he says.

Blue Dress sits me down in one of the chairs, and George begins pulling the pins from my hair, unwinding my braids. It is so strange to have a man touch me, I begin to tremble. I close my eyes and remember the soldiers with their big black boots. After my village burned, I was so afraid that the soldiers would come back and find me. There were stories about what they did to girls alone. I was so scared, that was the only reason I dared to walk away from my village, to walk away from the only place I'd ever known, to go to the city and send word to Lev.

I feel cold steel at the back of my neck. I freeze, too terrified to leap up and run away. I can only wait, in horror. And then: "All done," George says.

I open my eyes. My hair lies on the floor now, a dark brown carpet. This is so much less awful than what I thought might happen, that tears come into my eyes.

Blue Dress laughs.

"It does take a little getting used to," she says. "I remember when I first got my hair bobbed, I cried for hours. But it's *so* much easier. And just wait until your fiancé gets a look at you. He's been in America for a while, right? Believe me, this is what he expects."

Lev has been in America for two years, a lifetime, it seems— a time in which a lot of lives ended. What if he is a stranger to me now?

Blue Dress leads me back into the first room, where Green Dress and Yellow Dress *ooh* and *aah* some more. There's more brushing and fussing, and I'm getting a little tired of being their doll.

Enough playtime, I want to say. *Send me out to Lev or send me back to die, but stop toying with me.*

Then Blue Dress coos, "All right, all right, she's perfect now. Let her see!"

Green Dress hustles me toward another screen that turns out to have a huge mirror stretched across its panels. The other women cluster around. We all stand before the mirror and—

I have disappeared. This must be some sort of magic mirror, a trick mirror, because it gives back no reflection of me, only four butterfly-women: two blond and two dark-haired; one in green, one in blue, one in yellow, one in pink. The one in pink, strangely, is clutching a bundle of old, dirty, tattered rags.

The one in pink is me.

I stare, and the pink-dress woman goes goggle-eyed. I've seen very few mirrors in my lifetime: Shayna down the lane had a hand mirror she bought from a tinker once, but she was stingy about showing it around. Mostly I've seen my reflection only in ponds and lakes, rivers and streams. So how can I trust my eyes?

"Yes, that's you," Blue Dress says, as if she can read my mind. She giggles. "I love this part!"

I step forward and touch the glass. My reflected face is cold and smooth. I do not look like a girl who hid behind a tree, watching her entire village burn, watching the bayonets pass through her father, her mother, her sisters, her friends. I do not look like a girl who walked for days, without food, looking over her shoulder the entire way. I look like a butterfly, one of those creatures that danced and flitted above the meadow after the soldiers left—danced and flitted as if they did not care.

"I—" I say, but that is the only word I can manage.

The butterfly-women laugh and preen, spinning me around, showing me to myself from every angle. Then Yellow Dress steps away from the mirror.

"I'll just go check—" she says, walking out the door. She comes back a few minutes later and announces. "Yes, they say her young man is here."

Her words strike panic into my heart, and the pink butterfly-woman in the mirror goes pale. Here I am, playing with frippery and finery, and Lev is waiting, my whole life is waiting. My decision is waiting.

I tug at the buttons on the pink dress.

"I give back now," I say, trying to break away from the cluster of butterflies, trying to go back behind the screen. I wonder if they will trade me back, my hair in exchange for this foolish dress. But no, it's too late for that. Hair cannot be glued back on; what I've lost can't be returned.

"Oh, no," Blue Dress says, patting my hands away, rebuttoning everything I've managed to undo. "The dress is yours now. You keep."

"No money," I say, frustrated that butterflies can be so stupid.

"You don't have to pay," Blue Dress says. "We're a charity, here to help the poor immigrants from overseas. This is our gift to you. Gift."

I blink.

"Oh," I say.

"Come on!" Yellow Dress says, tugging on my hand. "Let's go see your beloved!"

The butterfly-women pull me out into a cavernous room that's crowded, like all of Ellis Island, with people who seem to be speaking every language known to man. The Dutch children have wooden shoes, and the Swedish women have elaborate headdresses, and the African men have skin as black as night. I don't see anyone who looks like me, but I wonder if there are any other girls here who have to make a decision like mine. If there were, I would ask them what they are going to do, because I don't know. I cannot think very well in this pink dress, in this huge room, in this hubbub of different tongues.

I see Lev before he sees me. He has gotten taller in America, and broader in the chest. I mistake him at first for his older brother, Kapel, but I know Kapel is dead. He was the only one I saw who tried to fight back against the soldiers.

"Lev," I say, and he stares at me.

"Anna?" he says.

I nod, but he does not seem to believe me. He blinks, as though he cannot make his eyes see me as separate from the butterfly-women who are clumped behind me, watching.

"They gave me this dress," I say. "So I could look American." I speak to him in our language, the language of our village. The words feel strange on my tongue, coming out with the extra twist of accent, of dialect, that I did not know people in my village had until I stopped hearing it in anyone else's voice.

But Lev talks the same way I do. I heard it just in the way he said, "Anna?" I feel a flutter of relief, that I am not completely alone in this roomful of strange languages, in this world full of strangers. Still, it has been so long since I have shared my language with anyone outside my own head that it feels too intimate now, as if Lev can know my thoughts. I feel myself blushing.

Slowly Lev raises his hand to touch my hair, just the tips where it ends.

"I used to dream about your hair," he murmurs sadly. "The way it blew in the breeze in the meadow, so free . . ."

And I see in his eyes that I have lost more than I thought. I did not realize that he has a decision to make, too. Maybe he said I could come only out of politeness, because they would not let me into America if I did not have a man here waiting. Maybe I will decide yes and he will decide no, all because of something silly like hair.

"Hair can grow back," I say impatiently.

He drops his hand, but he's still looking at me uncertainly.

"Is it true, then, what you wrote to me?" he asks. "Our village is gone? Everyone is gone?"

It is not that he doubts me, I think, but that he cannot believe it until he hears the words straight from my lips.

"Yes," I whisper, and somehow all the grief I've held off comes back. Lev is the only one in the world besides me who understands everything we lost. The only one who can mourn with me.

Lev's fingers brush my cheek, a comfort.

"But you escaped. . . ." he says softly.

"I was in the meadow with the sheep when the soldiers came. They did not see me. I went and hid and watched. . . ." Tears roll down my cheeks, the first tears I haven't brushed away or hidden. "Isn't it silly that the sheep saved my life? And when I sold them, it was enough money to bring me here. . . ."

Lev has a faraway look in his eyes.

"I was going to go back," he says. "When I had enough money, I was going to go home to my family. I was going to buy more land than anyone else in the village. More land and more sheep and more cows . . . And then—" He does not quite look at me. "Then I was going to marry you."

His words seem to fall into silence, as if all the other voices in this huge room have stopped their chatter. As if everyone else is as surprised as I am. Or as if my ears can no longer hear anything else when I am trying so hard to hear Lev, trying so hard to think . . . Everything seems different now, even the clods of dirt we threw at each other when we were ten. Even the reasons he left without saying good-bye.

"You can still marry me," I say. Am I giving permission? Am I saying yes? Am I too bold because of this silly pink dress? Because I don't look like myself, it's hard to remember how I'm supposed to act. "But you don't have to," I say quickly. "I can get a job, I can work, I can take care of myself. You don't have to take care of me."

"I know," Lev says. "But I want to. I want us to take care of each other."

He puts his arms around me, and I lean into the hug. And it's strange, even though he's gotten taller and broader, even though I'm wearing this silly dress, we fit together. I didn't expect this, or the sudden rush of emotion in my heart. The rush of hope. Of longing. Could it be—?

Someone sighs dreamily behind us—one of the butterfly-women. For a moment I forgot them, forgot my outlandish dress.

"I don't have to look like this," I say, tilting my head up so I can see Lev's face.

"Maybe I'll want you to," he says, laughing. "Sometimes."

So I have an answer, then, because of this dress. Lev and I have a chance at happiness. Suddenly I believe we'll be able to laugh together, sometimes, and dance, and act like Americans, as carefree as butterflies. We have a chance to share more than grief and memories, to fly beyond it all.

"Oooh," one of the butterfly-women squeals. "I just love happy endings."

She is still foolish. This is no ending, only a beginning. But as Lev slips his hand into mine and we look for the next line to stand in, to take the ferry away from Ellis Island, that is enough for me.

Joyce Sweeney was born in Dayton, Ohio. Her first novel, Center Line, *was chosen as the first annual Delacorte Prize winner. Since then, she has written eleven other novels, the latest of which,* Takedo *(Marshall Cavendish, 2004), was just selected by the American Library Association as a 2005 Quick Pick for Reluctant Readers. In addition to writing, Joyce also teaches creative writing workshops, which so far have produced twelve published authors. She lives in Coral Springs, Florida, with her husband, Jay, and cat, Macoco.*

ON "SOME CALL ME MAURICE": All writers have a "file" in their mind, of interesting stories and facts they pick up every day. When I lived in Dayton, I had a female hairdresser who told me the story of how she and her friends would go clubbing and pretend to be French—they said it drove guys wild! And even though she faked a very good accent, she didn't speak a word of French! I always thought that was the coolest thing. . . . When I heard about the anthology, I started thinking how much of our self-esteem comes from the image we create, and voilà! I had the story of Michael and how he learned in one day that confidence is just a game anyone can play.

René Saldaña, Jr., lives with his wife, Tina, their son, Lukas, and their cat, ISBN, in deep South Texas where he works as a teacher of English and creative writing at the University of Texas-Pan American. He has published two books of fiction: The Jumping Tree *and* Finding Our Way. *In addition, several of his poems, stories, articles, and book reviews have appeared or are forthcoming in* Every Man for Himself, Boys' Life, Face Relations, *and* READ, *among others. He also serves as the South Texas regional editor for* Texas Books in Review.

ON "NOT MUCH TO IT": I worked at a bookstore while attending school. I always thought it was so interesting to see what books customers were ordering. Don't get me wrong: I wasn't a biblio-Peeping-Tom. And I wasn't passing judgment. This practice worked more like a writing exercise for me: build a story around a book I least thought fit a customer. On top of this, I met some pretty wacky folks at the store. One such irritating customer expected a coworker to tend to her every whim. What struck me about her was that as ugly-spirited as she was, her hair and nails were immaculate. I put her together with a peculiar book, and although she is neither Becky nor Chela in my story, she began it all.

A respected poet and author of more than seventy books in many genres for children and young adults, **Marilyn Singer** *recently won a Lee Bennett Hopkins Poetry Award Honor Book citation for* Creature Carnival *(Hyperion, 2004). She has edited and contributed to three other anthologies besides this one:* Stay True: Short Stories for Strong Girls *(Scholastic, 1998);* I Believe in Water: Twelve Brushes with Religion *(HarperCollins, 2000); and* Face Relations: 11 Stories about Seeing Beyond Color *(Simon & Schuster, 2004). She lives in Brooklyn, NY, and Washington, CT, with her husband, Steven Aronson, their standard poodle, Oggi, and several other pets, including a talking starling. Please visit her Web site: www.marilynsinger.net*

ON "BEDHEAD RED, PEEKABOO PINK": I blame Clay Aiken and *American Idol* for this story. Along with millions of other folks, I was fascinated by the transformation of a nerdy guy into a rather handsome dude. It seemed to me that, although Clay might have been pleased with his new appearance, he didn't have much say in it. I began to wonder for what reasons a noncelebrity would want such a makeover. *Would he do it for his own self-esteem? Would he do it for someone he loved?* These questions led to others: What if that someone couldn't see what he looked like? *What if that someone was blind? Would a blind person want to go out with an unattractive date?* Whenever I ask that many questions, I have to try and answer them—and that to me is what fiction is all about.

Author of a dozen novels and many short stories, **Peni R. Griffin** *says she is an Air Force brat who settled in San Antonio, the most beautiful city in the world, is married to the most wonderful man in the world, and chose to have cats instead of children. Although she hopes eventually to write full-time, she currently does word processing for a real-estate appraisal* *firm in a building not unlike the one her heroine ascends in lieu of a mountain. Her most recent book,* **11,000 Years Lost,** *is a time-travel story about a girl who goes back in time and lives with mammoth hunters. "Written properly, any book will bring you closer to being who you really are," she says. "This book was more like a vision quest than anything I ever did before." Her Web site is: http://www.txdirect.net/users/griffin/0writing.htm*

ON "VISION QUEST": The concept of the makeover is that the person being made over is not good enough, and the person doing the makeover knows more about what she ought to be than the victim does.

This makes me want to vomit.

So I realized early that mine would have to be a reverse makeover story, in which someone discards an inauthentic persona and turns into herself. This is what adolescence is for in our extended-childhood society. The trouble is that humans, as social animals, know who we are by the way others respond to us. This gives each of us tremendous power over others and leaves us at the mercy of those around us, until we recognize our true core selves.

A story starts with a person and cannot be told without one; so I began with a girl who is a mirror to those around her, a different self for every individual in her life. She begins walking in a straight line because this is something I do myself when the stress is too bad. The importance of physical exhaustion to emotional clarity is central to the transformative experience. So I set her off walking, writing a paragraph or so at a time on my lunch hour, and when she got to the top of the building and came face to face with herself, I did some research on the creature she manifested as, and there we were, at the start of her journey.

Joseph Bruchac is a writer and traditional storyteller whose work has been widely published—from books of poetry and novels for young readers to articles in magazines such as **National Geographic.** *His numerous honors include the Virginia Hamilton Award and the Lifetime Achievement Award from the Native Writers Circle of the Americas. He lives in upstate New York with his wife, Carol. His Web site is: www.josephbruchac.com*

ON "WABI'S EARS": My writing often draws on the oral traditions of my Abenaki Indian ancestors. Wabi, or "White Owl," is the name of a traditional Abenaki folk hero, and there are many Abenaki stories of transformation such as this one in which an animal becomes a person or vice versa. The boundary between the human world and the animal world is much more permeable in all Native cultures. Such tales, though, are always told in third person. The idea of doing it as a first person narration and seeing things through the eyes of the owl who becomes a person led me to this story.

Terry Trueman was born in Birmingham, Alabama, but grew up in Seattle. He has degrees in applied psychology and in creative writing. The father of two sons, Henry and Jesse, Terry currently makes his home with his wife, Patti, in Spokane, Washington, where he has lived since 1974.

His first novel, Stuck in Neutral, *was a Printz Honor recipient. He revisits the indelible characters from this book in* Cruise Control, *his third novel—the powerful story of a family torn apart by disability and divorce. His fourth novel,* No Right Turn, *will be published by HarperCollins in winter, 2006.*

Terry's hobbies include his Sea Ray boat and his 1976 Corvette Stingray, a photo of which can be found on his Web site: www.terrytrueman.com

ON "HONESTLY, TRUTHFULLY": This particular story is a blend of two elements I'd been thinking about a lot; the first is honesty versus lying. I'd been considering this on multiple levels, but with particular fascination for where does "lying" begin and normal socialized behavior end? As a convert to Catholicism at the age of fifty, while barely ever letting go of my agnosticism, I find the entire world of lying interesting.

The other element played with in my story again relates to socialized versus inappropriate behaviors, and to be honest I stole my approach to the idea for "Skungy Day" from a novel I love by William Kotzwinkle, *The Fan Man*. Writing for teens allows an author to go back to the basics, the foundations of issues which we older adults take for granted—such as what is appropriate/inappropriate; this is one of the things I enjoy most about my work.

Jess Mowry was born in Mississippi in 1960 and raised in Oakland, California. In 1988 he began writing stories for and about the kids in his West Oakland neighborhood. Since then, his stories have appeared in numerous magazines and anthologies, including ZYZZYVA, Obsidian II, The Los Angeles Times Magazine, Brotherman, In the Tradition, Stay True, *and* Face Relations. *His essays have appeared in* The Nation *and* The San Francisco Chronicle. *He has written seven books, which have been published in eight languages, as well as a screenplay for a produced feature-length film based on his novel,* Way Past Cool. *He works with disadvantaged kids in Oakland and mentors young writers. Read about him at:* http://timoun.tripod.com/

ON "THE RESURRECTION": "The Resurrection" seemed to fit the theme of this anthology because isn't Death the ultimate makeover? No matter what we've done with (or to) our bodies—changed our hairstyle, gone on a diet, gotten pierced or tattooed, whitened our teeth, suffered with braces, had a nip or a tuck here and there—Death is never impressed when He meets us; and we'll all look about the same in our coffins. But, our spirits go on to become something new, and then we all become beautiful, and by much higher standards than Hollywood's. I'm not sure if anyone is better off dead, but in the case of Sniffles in this story, as with so many other kids like him, it sometimes seems easier to die than to live when no one on earth will help make you over.

Of her seven novels for young adults, **Norma Howe's** *favorite is* Blue Avenger Cracks the Code, *the second book in her Blue Avenger trilogy.* (The Adventures of Blue Avenger, *the first book in the series, was an ALA Best Book for Young Adults and a finalist for the California Young Reader Medal.) Her secret dream, she says, is to one day see her three Blue Avenger books published in a paperback omnibus volume. Log on to her Web site at www.members.aol.com/normahowe to read more about her favorite book, plus a complete list of all her books, together with their reviews and some rather intimate details about her life and writing. You can also write to her at P.O. Box 980672, West Sacramento, CA 95798-0672 for a free, homemade autographed bookmark.*

ON "BAZOOKA JOE AND THE CHAOS KID": My husband (and high school sweetheart), Bob, and I are the parents of six children and the grandparents of eight. That explains why writing a description of Frank's disastrous room was duck soup. I'm fearless enough to confess that most of my writing springs either from my own experiences or those that I've personally observed in others, even though that admission sometimes sparks some wild speculation on the part of my friends and family.

My first dozen published "works" were true confession stories (i.e., "Trapped in My Boyfriend's Bedroom," *Modern Love,* Feb. 1972). Aside from "Bazooka Joe" I have written only one other short story since my true confession days. You can read it in Michael Cart's 2003 anthology called *Necessary Noise.* I find the short story format quite confining, since in my novels I enjoy the freedom of going off on little tangents that most readers enjoy, but which one sourpuss reviewer called "unnecessary asides." Consequently, the editor of this anthology was obliged to guide me through four revisions, patiently sifting out the superfluous characters and unrelated riffs. (Oh, but I do so miss those bagpipes in the second draft.)

Marina Budhos is the author of short stories, adult novels, and a young adult nonfiction book, Remix: Conversations With Immigrant Teenagers. *Her first young-adult novel,* Ask Me No Questions, *will be published by Simon & Schuster in 2006. An assistant professor of English at William Paterson University, Marina is married to writer/editor Marc Aronson. They are the proud parents of two boys, Sasha and Raphael. Marina's Web site is: http://www.marinabudhos.com/*

ON "THE PLAN": This is a story that just popped out at me. I'd always wanted to do a piece about a kid of ambiguous ethnic and racial background whose mother wants to fake it in Hollywood as his older sister. They were definitely characters that were rattling around inside my head. Then I visited a screenwriter friend in California whose daughter is a model. The setting of the apartment, her daughter's portfolio, the vibe of selling a "look" in the media made the atmosphere very real to me. By the time I sat down to write, the whole story was formed in my head.

Evelyn Coleman's children's and young-adult books have received numerous honors, including Parents' Choice *Honor Book; the* Smithsonian Most Outstanding Children's Book Title; American Booksellers Association's Pick of the Lists; Publishers Weekly's Cuffie Award; and Notable Chil-*

dren's Trade Books in the Field of Social Studies. Evelyn is the recipient of the 38th Annual Georgia Author of the Year Award, Children/Young Adult Literature; the King Baudouin/Belgium Cultural Exchange Fellowship; the Atlanta Mayor's Fellowship; and the North Carolina's Arts Council's Fiction Fellowship. She was also honored in 2003 by the Black & Latino Caucus of the NCTE. You can find out more about her at: www.evelyncoleman.com/childhome1.htm

ON "LUCKY SIX": I have met several young women in Atlanta, beautiful, smart, and savvy, who work as what they call "exotic dancers" and what I call "strippers." It was a puzzle to me how they functioned, living in a shelter, dancing, and at the same time going to high school. After some discussion it became clear to me that money was the motivating factor in all cases. These girls wanted a better life. Each of them had come from dysfunctional homes, where oftentimes certain sexual mores were considered "normal"; however, it was clear to me that when pressed, these young women did not want to do this type dancing but felt they had to do it in order to survive. I wanted to write a story where, at least on paper, one of them escapes.

Margaret Peterson Haddix is the author of numerous books for teens, including Running Out of Time, Escape from Memory, Just Ella, Take-offs and Landings, *the* Among the Hidden *series, and her newest,* Double Identity. *Her books have won an International Reading Association's Children's Book Award, an ALA Top Ten Best Books for Young Adults citation, and many state readers' choice awards. She lives in Ohio with her family.*

ON "BUTTERFLIES": Several years ago when I was visiting the museum at Ellis Island, one exhibit struck me as particularly bizarre and poignant. It depicted the efforts of various aid societies to give immigrants new clothes and updated hairdos so they'd fit in in America. The photos on the wall showed frumpy, worn-looking peasant women and girls transformed into 1920s flappers. But, to me, their eyes seemed to say, "This is not who we really are. Don't you know what we've been through?" I wondered if the makeovers were always as welcome as the glowing captions made it seem. And I knew that someday I would write about one of those girls.